Worlds Beyond the Cloud

John Albrecht

ALL RIGHTS RESERVED

No part of this book may be reproduced or transmitted in any form or by any means, electronic or mechanical, including photocopying, recording, or by any information storage and retrieval system, without permission in writing from the author, except in the case of brief quotations embodied in reviews.

Publisher's Note:

This is a work of fiction. All names, characters, places, and events are the work of the author's imagination.

Any resemblance to real persons, places, or events is coincidental.

Solstice Publishing - http://www.solsticeempire.com/

Copyright 2020 – John Albrecht

For Sharon

The Star Spring

Breathless beyond all expectation, the six crew members of the spacecraft *Star Wing*, The United Jurisdictions of Earth spacecraft sent aloft twelve years ago, now gazed at a perfect image of Proxima Centauri, Earth's closest star. Being a red dwarf $1/7^{th}$ the size of Earth's sun, normally the sight would not overwhelm. Yet at this moment, by happenstance, a blazing solar flare shot out, curling around it. So the star, deep red, lit up by searing flames, proved a wondrous sight.

Good thing the *Star Wing's* enormous solar sail, a mile long and a half mile wide at its base, had been partly furled. For this unexpected bombardment of photons might have set her off course and interfered with their orbital deceleration. And what a wonder that sail, propelled by the Sun's light photons. Then, entering the dark depths of space, a hyper-laser filled the sail with force. The spacecraft itself had two main components: first a train-like fuselage where the crew worked, second a rotating donut shaped structure which produced gravity for the crew's living quarters. But now, the saga of that twelve year voyage, with its revelations of inter-stellar space and human inner workings, faded from thought. For here before them now what they'd lived for all those years.

Appropriate maneuvers executed, the crew manned stations for the next and most crucial maneuver, locking into orbit around Proxima Centauri b, the star's only planet. Soon they orbited that Earth-sized world, now enveloped in clouds. Yet even while close to its sun, their instruments read its temperature as cool. For this planet's sun, small but densely compacted, shined much less brightly than Earth's.

Next day, the landing party entered Descent Vehicle One. Timed with precision, the craft touched down. With carbon dioxide levels high but other parameters balanced, wearing oxygen masks the explorers debarked. After twelve years in the black void of space, they practically breathed in these new vistas, like a sponge diver taking a breath again after a marathon dive.

Recovering from this effect, as First Mate Dan Stafford looked around he saw a stark plateau. To the west, rocky peaks stretched north to south, reddish in tone under a greyish blue sky. Turning eastward, beyond low cliffs he sighted a body of water, nature unknown. Next he beheld the sun of this world, so close and yet with subdued light. But even while he took this in, clear skies dimmed as cloud mass returned, appearing out of nowhere. Next these clouds turned luminous, faintly lighting up the lands below.

"Phew! Some place!" Dan said, breaking the silence.

"Yes, it is," Boatswain Aashi Stafford agreed, "with skies which change like we change a sweater. What could explain this effect, do you think?"

"Hard to say, Aashi, hard to say...although with two thousand times the solar wind here than on Earth, I'm guessing it may penetrate this planet's magnetic field from time to time and so cause substorms, these energizing the atmosphere, and possibly helping to drive this unusual weather pattern so that–"

"Driving the weather like a real wind would, but far more covertly, it makes for an odd connection between two separate systems, sun and planet."

"Thanks for completing my thought for me, Aashi, saved me a bit of work."

"Sorry to cut you off, Dan, but how fascinating that sudden cloud shift. But with lulls in the solar wind, skies here clear up."

"When you two are done sky gazing, we've got work to do," Captain Grieg cut in.

"Aw come on, Captain, admit it, you were just as blown away as us for our first minutes in this new world."

"Well, it's an old world now, three minutes old. Let's get going."

And so they surveyed the site for their base. A few days later a dome would be inflated from a liquid chemical base, producing a huge bubble. Under that hardened dome they would next set up their quarters, oxygen and water at first to be had from crushed rocks.

Next day, with the mother ship on auto pilot, all worked to erect their tiny new world under a dome some two hundred yards across. Living quarters tight but snug, hydroponic gardens would soon add a welcome Earth feel. For this planet, while having a certain raw beauty, felt to the eyes as a finger drawn over a saw blade. So the small space comprising their home would form a green cushion to blunt this effect. On a more practical level, a natural flow of oxygen from the gardens would replenish their dome.

Next, exploration forays began in earnest, these conducted by teams of two, Dan and Aashi setting out first. Dan, naturally drawn to the sea, found this one vast yet stifled. For this sea carbonated, no life worked its way through the depths. No refreshing breeze flowed in, only occasional gusts of carbon dioxide. Still, as a sea, Dan felt it alive in a way.

Soon they discovered how sea and sky related, the sea's carbon dioxide rising to help facilitate the unusual sky/cloud dynamic. Later they discovered active fissures on the planet's seabed, giving off carbonic acid. This is what they'd expected, as mother ship instruments had detected fissures filled with cooling magma beneath the planet's crust. All in all, an odd type of world.

So then, as information began to accrue, Captain Grieg called for a project summit meeting, in the open garden space facing the sunrise. By now, with the aid of stimulus lights, lush plants gave the spot the feel of a long lost resort of forgotten-in-time Far East tourists. The crew though, not on the outside looking in, felt the allure of such growth. Then too, their strict Captain Grieg had allowed Doctor Solander to make cucumber wine, something he assured the crew good for health. So, while sipping the surprisingly tasty stuff, they discussed what they'd learned to date.

"I agree with our captain," Cindy Grieg Lochart began. "So far, this planet presents us with empty footprints to track."

"Only because you're his wife you agree," Doctor Solander smiled while sipping more wine. "As for me, well, it's only just begun in this world, a fresh clean slate."

"Hear hear!" Marsha Solander agreed, "I vote with our doctor. We've got miles to go before we sleep in this place, metaphorically speaking, that is. What do you two think?" she added, turning to Dan and Aashi.

"Well," Dan tactfully replied, "what our captain says is true, on the face of it. I mean, now we know life doesn't exist on this planet."

"And yet," Aashi picked up the ball, "and yet we two, at least, still have a lingering sense that all is not as it outwardly appears to be. Oh, at first I doubted, but then something clicked. In other words, fellow crew members, while we have numbers that neatly add up so far, we have others which don't. To my mind, at least, this means the door remains open for something unforeseen to pass through."

"Maybe that door is opening up now!" Dan exclaimed, while gazing through the dome at the sky. As he spoke, the others saw something unforeseen in the works. For it appeared as if a second solar flare had erupted on the sun's surface, larger than the preceding one, judging by its effects on the sky. Normal air currents darkening roiled, and started to glow. This cloud mass next moved overhead. Flecks of faint light appeared to combine into swirling units, now self-propelled.

"My God, what can they be?" Captain Grieg spoke for them all. "I swear, those tiny flecks of light clustering up appear to be living things in the sky. But that's not possible...just can't be! Must be just an appearance...goes against all our readings to date. Even so, one of those things must be brought down for a closer look."

Having said this, while the rest of the crew watched on in stunned silence, their captain donned an oxygen mask, communicator and handgun. The temperature around 15° Celsius, out he strode to obtain a specimen. Finally taking a shot as one came into range, with odd circular motions it spun to the ground. Smiling now, the captain fetched his prize and inspected it closely. But then right above him, those random blots of light did an amazing thing. They appeared to swirl at first and next join together, forming one large and threatening whole. Quickly sensing the danger, Dan picked up his communicator.

"Captain, look above you! You're in danger! Get rid of that thing in your hands. Put it on the ground and get back in here quick! Somehow, they know what you've done."

Alerted to the danger now, the captain complied. Back in the dome, the threatening configuration above descended to the fallen entity and somehow inhaled it. This done, it withdrew from the base perimeter and broke down again into small units, which remained in motion near the surface. About thirty minutes later, changing the tone of their glowing, ascending, they faded from sight. The crew, stunned by this unknown display, for several moments more strove for composure.

"So," Captain Grieg spoke first, "just how does one describe an encounter like that?"

"One describes it as a trigger?" Aashi suggested.

"Meaning?"

"Meaning it has just triggered a cluster of associations in my mind. I'm assuming that all of you also have lots of thoughts bouncing around about now."

"Okay, Aashi, not a bad response. But besides the pending event reconstruction session, what would you suggest we do now?"

"Well, since we have no specimen to examine, Captain, could you at least describe it to us?"

"Yes, well, with the limited time I had to evaluate the thing, what pops into my mind now is the thought of a flying jellyfish, hmm, or more precisely, floating jellyfish. The one I held had been hit, right?"

"Yes, nice shot, too, Captain," Doctor Solander put in. "But, well, what I noticed after you apparently hit your target was the circular motions it made, sort of like a–"

"Like a balloon turned loose after being inflated?"

"Yes, something like that."

"That's because those creatures appear to have the quality first of having thin membranes for bodies, and second, being inflated for buoyancy, apparently for living in the sky. So punctured as that one was, down it went while the others floated above."

"Apparently taking note of what you'd done," the doctor added.

"Which seems entirely strange if they're composed of thin membranes alone, a large component of brainless jellyfish. And like jellyfish, they also appear to have tentacles…oh, not so large and developed as a jellyfish, but still there, the purpose of which remains unknown."

"But wait." Marsha picked up the ball. "Didn't any of you notice how before combining into one thing, they dived into the ground, touched lightly and then rose again?"

"Ah," Aashi responded, "and so number one, we have inflated, buoyant, creatures um, wanting to descend? Nearing the ground with tentacles, perhaps to grasp tiny pebbles?"

"To use as ballast," Dan sliced in, "lessening their buoyancy enough to allow them to hover about at low altitude, in this case apparently in preparation for an attack."

"Or in other cases allowing them to hover at low altitude to do something else…"

"Okay, gang, nice bits of observation. And like Aashi said, the trigger is the key here, in more ways than one. So, creatures that live in the air, composed of thin, inflated membranes, that first appear as tiny light flecks, assemble into blobs which in turn can assemble into one larger cloud-like unit, come out of nowhere when a major solar flare hits this planet."

"Yes, yes, good, Captain, good. And the atmosphere at our level is composed largely of carbon dioxide…higher up there's oxygen, hydrogen, and a few other trace gases. Are they plant-creatures which live in the air firstly as cellular clusters that due to lack of energy are dormant for periods of time? Then, stirred to life by the required particle inflow, these cellular clusters assemble into the plant-creatures. These in turn move down to where they can find the quantities of carbon dioxide they need to live. Ah, and their initial buoyancy brought about as they fill up with hydrogen in the upper atmosphere."

"And," Dan continued, "as the solar flare energy and solar wind combined manage to drive them downward, they *release* a bit of their hydrogen, dive for the ground to pick up tiny pebbles, this small added weight allowing them to linger as photosynthesis takes place…then dropping the pebbles when done, they return to the sky."

"Well now, congratulations, boys and girls. Who says your years of observational training were wasted?" Captain Grieg capped it all. "Now, to be honest, in space you guys appeared somewhat boneheaded to me, but then again, an albatross looks like shit on the ground, elegant in flight. So with your scintillating flights of fancy here we have at least a visually based theory to go by. But you know, somehow, someway, we have to get a specimen...but then again, the attack...ah, but what the hell could such creatures do to cause us harm?"

"Do you really want to find out?" Dr. Solander spoke for them all.

"Yes, that is the question, of course..."

"Yes, and a pointed question at that," Dan added. "But now, one more point here regarding the nature of these things. Wind, first powerful solar wind from this sun, combined with a fiery solar flare, jets through the short distance of space to this planet where both instantly intermingle, to some degree, with our planet's atmosphere, becoming one in a way, and not just as a metaphor."

"Ah, but Dan," Aashi replied, "to add to your idea, consider how in this case, these creatures, so largely linked to the sun for their origin, make Proxima Centauri's emissions a flowing spring of potential life, in a sense, quite the opposite of what many believe about these types of solar activities."

"Huh, so it would seem, at least in our one observed case," the captain noted. "But I don't think we can state it as a universal principle at this point, crew. And look, let's wrap this session up and get back to assigned tasks. At the right time, this episode will repeat for our further edification."

And so the rest of their day unfolded, back on track after the startling encounter. That evening though would be a special event.

"Well, crew," Doctor Solander began, mellowed out after dinner, "you know how we've been trained to look straight ahead only – good advice to give tightrope walkers in space like us. Yes, look forward only...because one glance back or aside can unravel the most raveled of minds so far into space as we are. But today, right at this moment, I have to look back. Yes, now I look back to our home, an invisible dot in space going round a fairly bright star, quite a ways off. What about that gulf we've crossed, light years wide? What kind of wind surfers are we, anyway? Skittering first though the Oort Cloud, that great frozen sea, and on though the depths not of space alone, but through the depths of time and being...to bring us to this forlorn star, collapsed from its former bright glory, and now sit on a planet with such a strange parent...apparently giving this planet life of a sort...

"What this all means to me, my friends, is that distance is crucial here. Not raw distance alone, but the distance too in our minds that connects a past event to daily life. Yes, a memory fades with the distance we travel through time and space, or does it? My memories of home may be compressed, so distant now in my mind as well as in sheer space. But maybe memories don't fade away, maybe they just get more compact until they collapse into points. And then, like stars in a night sky, they brightly burn as beacons, guiding us home."

"True, Dr. Solander," Dan agreed, "and how I long too for home, and not on the range for me. Yeah, I could tell you stories of the North Carolina coast that would put waves in your hair, those memories stirred by the sight of our sea here. But enough of the memory lane stuff. 'Cause right here and now, I'm going to predict that by the end of our mission, we'll feel a pang of loss for this world, odd as that sounds now. But it's only natural to internalize a new place, even an odd place like this. Ah, but about these lifeforms of ours...well, let me tell you, some noteworthy discovery lurks here, a marvelous one, in fact. Linked to a sun and a planet for life, how could it be otherwise?"

The Star Web

With the discovery of a new lifeform, the crew of the *Star Wing* knew hard work lay ahead. Their first task clear, they had to grasp the essence of this new type of life. But since they had no sample to analyze, this goal was blocked. Sitting in their meeting room after breakfast, they prepared to tackle this issue. Then, as sunrise approached, all heads turned as eyes affixed to the sight. And, while no radiant sun like Earth's, that old red star had rays of beauty, too.

"So," Captain Grieg began, turning away from the life-giving star, "about this lack of data on our new lifeform: we know they go berserk if we try to grab one for analysis. And, from a distance, our instruments can't read them. So, the question is, just how do we work our way out of this conundrum?"

"By beating that conundrum?" Dan suggested.

"Just knew I could count on you, Dan, for a flippant remark."

"No flippancy intended, Captain Grieg. I only mean to say that a conundrum, if conceived of in the right way, represents a working model of sorts."

"Now *that* is going to take some fancy footwork to explain. Start dancing."

"Okay. No pressure, right? Anyway, think here of the idea of paradox, a construct which works well in philosophy."

"Works well in...aw hell, let's just fast forward through yet another one of your crappola expositions, shall we, Dan? And I still say I should just grab one of the damn things so we can study it up close."

"Oh, but Captain Grieg," Aashi cut in, "as you just noted, this lifeform reacts in a dangerous way when threatened. So, if we could lure it close enough for our instruments to read, that would be a safer course of action."

"Now look, Aashi, if our instruments tell us squat from a distance, how much better would they work up close and personal?"

"Wait!" Marsha piped in, sitting up. "Captain Grieg, you first of all labeled these creatures flying jellyfish. But why not consider them birds of a sort?"

"But they're not birds, Marsha, nothing like that."

"Oh now, think about it, Captain Grieg," Marsha persisted, "these creatures, like birds, have to descend to feed, like real birds for seeds or bread. These jellified versions descend to feed on carbon dioxide, which, on this planet, is at concentrated levels close to the ground."

"Tell us something we don't know."

"I'm getting to that. So, back on Earth, what brings skittish pigeons to the ground to feed, first of all, but next to cozy up to big hungry humans?"

"Pigeons, you say? Damn flying rats! I hate those things, Marsha. Wrong analogy to use."

"Wait!" Dan interjected. "If I'm not mistaken, Marsha, you're about to suggest we make a carbon dioxide bird feeder, attract them with a concentrated dose of their favorite CO_2 treat to come close to our dome, in semi-friendly fashion, close enough for our instruments to take readings of their anatomies."

"Yes! Congratulations, Dan. That's the plan and –"

"– it just might work," Aashi completed Marsha's sentence.

And so, when the next solar flare came around and the dormant creatures woke up, combined into blobs and then their cloud-like unit, the crew of the *Star Wing* shot a jet of CO_2 into the air near the western side of their dome. Remarkably, it did in fact draw the creatures down. Seeming not to show any alarm this time as they neared humans, they began to do their thing close to the ground.

Then, when sated on their carbon dioxide meal, they did another odd thing – they lingered on, sensing their human company. During this brief interaction, crew members' conscious thoughts began to merge with unconscious thoughts and dream-like imagery. Aashi, in fact, began to hear rhythmic sounds like some kind of music, a type of pulse that passed between the creatures. Then, the whole crew began to sense information being passed between the air jellyfish as their cluster began to ascend. As they did, almost as if by a gravitational tug, the thoughts and imagery in their own minds began to rise, like upward blossoming clouds, roiling in beautiful patterns before fading out.

"Whoa!" Dan exclaimed with a startled look. "Am I the only one to have just had some kind of ah, experience?"

"Yeah, I did too, for one," the captain replied. "So these plant-animal things – ha! At least we know what kind of plant we're dealing with."

"A little funny, Captain," Aashi noted, "but as I'm sure you're aware, quite off the mark. That experience – it was as if certain forces induced what went on in us, real external forces, our minds the sea, those creatures combined the moon."

"And look, everyone, look at our instruments!" Cindy exclaimed. "They show nothing but a rhythmic pulse! My God, it's as if this joining together of their individual forms equals an as yet indiscernible entity with some kind of internal functions. Yet the only evidence we have of its existence instrument-wise is a rhythmic pulse."

"But there's more, Captain Grieg," Doctor Solander put in. "Now, what I'm going to say may sound a little flaky, maybe like something Dan would say…just kidding, Dan, but your Zen paradox stuff and your latest bit here…"

"Okay, okay, forget that and tell us what you think."

"Alright, here's the gist of my thought: that gravitational tug we felt in our minds, whatever its true nature, carries a charge of some kind, though maybe our instrument not designed to read it. And now the clouds here, as we know, at times like this carry a negative charge. So, here it is: the creatures, or um, the *united* creature, strikes the ground like slow motion lightning, in a way, at least…which leads me to believe that it passes on to the planet itself some kind of, some kind of…"

"Some kind of message?" Aashi suggested.

"Ha, you know, that's not what I was going to say, Aashi, I was going to say that the creature passes on a negative charge to this planet's surface, like lightning does on Earth, but let's go with your idea for the moment and see where it leads…or, if the creature passes on no actual message, maybe it's some kind of temporary *link*, yeah, a link of some kind that makes atmosphere and planet one, at least for a moment."

"Oh, yes, great insight, Doctor Solander. And so, by extension of your thought, the solar flare striking the atmosphere in a sense links our new sun to the moment of that linking of sky and planet…"

"Sun, space, atmosphere, planet, all linked as one for a moment?" Dan added while tugging his chin.

"Okay, gang," the captain chimed in, "Doctor Solander's wine is on the menu tonight. After this jumble of thoughts, that stuff by comparison grounds us!"

"Aha, Captain!" Marsha piped in out of the blue. "Could it be that this planet may well represent a case where a non-predator ecosystem has developed?"

"Well hell, Marsha, will that segue of yours eventually merge back into our foregoing discussion? Because if it doesn't…"

"Yes it will, Captain Grieg. I'm not quite sure how at this point, other than to suggest that the unification of cosmic elements under discussion, in my mind, at least, points in that direction."

"Anything else?"

"Well, I know it's an odd notion and certainly stands our conventional understanding of life sciences on its head, but think about it: this planet has an intensely isolated feeling about it. Add to this the solar connection of our new lifeform giving it an entirely new dynamic, more linear, if you will, and less convulsed by the bumps and detours that in my mind, at least, partly explain the need for predators to evolve, predators being creatures that pick up the scraps of life, so to speak.

"On the other hand, on Proxima Centauri b, for reasons yet unfathomed, our lifeform appears to deal with this scrap problem on its own. Recall how they hovered over you, Captain, until you dropped their fallen one, and mysteriously absorbed it into their own substance when you pulled away."

Captain Grieg, speechless for a change, considered this thought.

"Yeah, but...never mind. Continue, Marsha."

"Ah yes, and think too, Captain, of desulforudis vindicator, a bacterium discovered some time ago in the cracks of a South African gold mine, a species of bacteria which represents a wholly self-sustaining ecosystem living without predation."

"A very isolated case! But ah, if you have anything else to add, feel free."

"What we're trying to say, Captain Grieg, is that with the discovery of an inexplicable life form..."

"...we're just trying to make it splickable," Aashi added, smiling.

"Right. Well, what about our instrumentation angle?"

"Sorry Captain," Marsha replied, "our instruments pick up rhythmic pulsations only."

"What kind of lifeform would leave so meager a footprint?"

"Maybe the problem here, Captain Grieg, is that we think of such a reading as primitive, this word obscuring something that, while simple and seemingly only partially developed, could in fact represent 500 million years of evolution, or even longer, for all we know to date."

"Right. Well hell crew, I think we've got more than enough material here to reflect on for further discussion. Maybe by then key issues will have come into sharper focus. Meeting's adjourned."

So then, the next few weeks on Proxima Centauri b unfolded in less dramatic ways, once the big surprise of the place began to recede. They would just have to wait for the next life-form appearance for more information. In the meantime, exploration continued apace, Dan and Aashi's assignment the sea. Playfully named the Soda Sea, Dan especially sensed in its untold story. And so, with Aashi by his side one day as waves swished up the beach, the unforeseen happened.

"Oh my God, Aashi, look at that! A meteor shower like never seen on Earth! The sky – just look at it sizzle! If a big one hits the sea, we could be swept away by a tidal wave!"

As calmly as possible then, they exited the beach and headed for home. On the plateau with the base not far off, the meteor shower ended. But as the still jumpy pair entered their gardens for a dose of calming green, they were greeted by cold stony faces. For just moments before Captain Grieg had informed the crew their mother ship had just been demolished.

Stunned silence prevailed for the rest of the day, each crew member weaving between denial and despair. Eating in silence as well, only with a glass of wine each did they begin to unwind.

"Well, it could be worse, guys," Aashi spoke first. "We still have our lives and our minds, and a well-stocked base. We could thrive here for years."

"Of futile exploration, accumulating data that no one on Earth will ever read," Marsha said while pouring herself some more wine.

"But Captain Grieg," Doctor Solander objected, "is not some kind of rescue mission possible?"

"Now now, Doctor Solander, surely you haven't forgotten the waiver you signed to become a part of this crew, have you? By doing so we all acknowledged the risks, and absolved the agency from fault should just such an occurrence as this actually happen. I mean, let's face it, dangerous variables go with a mission of this nature, space being what it is, a vast unknown. And we're not merely marooned on an island as in times past. We are lost in the absolute depths of space, and time, even...almost too vast to contemplate, and devouring a big chunk of our lives even if we had been able to return at the end of three years. Even worse, with us unable to transmit a message through the vast stretch of deep space involved, well, you figure it out. Still, my friends, still...think of what we can continue to learn here and store in indestructible files. Think of the knowledge...eventually someone else will land here, find our treasure trove."

Not thrilled by this notion just then, the crew nonetheless decided to enjoy the evening. But with the point of their mission now gone, next day their feet felt like lead. In this listless state then, while on their way home from another Soda Sea expedition, eyes downcast, Dan and Aashi stopped dead in their tracks when they looked up. With a gasp and hands to her chest, Aashi was the first to grasp the event.

"Who, who are you?" she asked in shock and wonder. There before the two stood a man uniquely attired, especially for a dim and distant planet. For he wore a cape of sorts draped back from a type of breastplate overlaid with cunning designs. The face of the man was long, his forehead rounded. Unable to tell if his bald head real or shaved, the stunned pair next looked into his eyes. They sparkled with unfeigned delight, easing their heart rates.

"If you would be so kind as to invite me into your quarters, I will explain all."

Soon all had gathered in their garden meeting place, the plants of Earth reassuring in this alien presence. Yet somewhat alien though he appeared, none got the sense of an unfathomable other before them. Captain Grieg, on the other hand, mind firmly fixed on the alien aspect of this encounter, took a more cautious approach. For as the former *Star Wing's* captain, he was keenly aware both of his responsibility for any possible danger as well as the civilities such an unprecedented occasion called for. So then, bidding his guest be seated, he offered him a glass of the good doctor's wine. The crew appeared stunned by the simple sight of the alien smiling as he accepted the wine, as if aware of its symbolic meaning. Picking up his cue, the captain, raising his glass, proposed a toast.

"To our new found friend and guest of honor," he warmly intoned, all then raising their glasses. Glasses set back on the table, Captain Grieg let his sense of wonder get the better of him.

"I can scarcely believe what we've all just done," he said, hand passing over his face. "This is vastly beyond a merely memorable moment. The word eternal comes to mind, odd as that notion seems to me most of the time."

"And um, if you don't mind my asking," Aashi boldly cut in, "how did you, sir, know of our custom of toasting?"

As Captain Grieg glowered the alien only smiled.

"I have no direct experience with your…custom, as you say. But the intention of your gesture speaks louder than words."

"Ah, an idiom of ours," Dan added.

"It is really? A simple turn of phrase has special meaning for you?"

Feeling the need to seize back his leadership role, Captain Grieg laid down the law.

"I would ask all crew present to act with restraint. This is not one of your high school reunions, you know. We stand now on the frontier of being to being interaction. This being so, if I ask for comments from you, feel free to join in. Otherwise, put a sock in it, to use an Earth expression our kind can speedily grasp."

Silence then enfolded the crew like a cloud.

"That's better. So now, let me inform you, honored guest, that my name is Maximilian Grieg, Captain Maximilian Grieg, that is to say, although our ship sadly lost. May I ask you your name?"

"My name, in your language, would be rendered Bretori. And you might be interested to learn that my people, the Kworthi, each have unique, unrepeated names which all end with the same character."

"Thank you for that um, intimate sharing of information, Bretori. But now, maybe the most burning question on all our minds here is…how did you find us? Was it by design, or did it just happen? The second question, ah, or maybe it should be the first…is where did you come from?"

"In your terms, I come from a planet about 107 of your light years from here, a planet we call Orothi Une. I know too that your home planet is 4.5 light years away from here."

"Ah, you must have amazing spacecraft…to have come so far…"

"Yes, we do have amazing spacecraft, but I did not come here in one of them."

"Really? That's um, a stunning statement. If not by ship then, how did you get here?"

"I did not really get here. As we speak, I am also on my home planet."

"Okaaay, let me think about that for a moment…"

"On your planet, you would refer to my means of appearing here as bi-location."

"Ah yes, I think...being two places at once..."

"Yes, an obscure phenomenon, but not unknown on your planet."

"Captain Grieg, may I speak?" Dan asked.

"Hey, be my guest at this point. I need to think about this for a moment."

"Bretori, I, I do know something of what you speak of. There have been reports of this baffling phenomenon on Earth – people simultaneously appearing in two distinct locations. The mechanism at work may never be known, and most of our scientists dismiss this idea out of hand...oh, but now, the distances involved in what you say are so vast, vastly beyond any reports of bi-location on Earth..."

"Vast indeed. So you wonder first at the missing piece of logic here, the fact that on your Earth a person who bi-locates needs to have knowledge of the other location. Otherwise this phenomenon, as you say, would not be possible."

"That is one of my questions."

"Yes. So let me tell you that I *did* have knowledge of this location, even though I have never been here before. The creatures in the atmosphere, you see, are the link."

"Really? How does it work?"

"It is really rather simple. These creatures represent, or are a manifestation of, the instantaneous interconnection of our universe. This instantaneous interconnectedness defies sheer distance and the velocities involved in going from one place to another. So these creatures you have encountered – through that moment of contact you experienced with them, you too became 'hooked up,' as your kind would say, with this vast web of cosmic interconnectedness, and so known to me, along with your location. And, when your ship was destroyed, instinct informed these creatures of your distress. And so they transmitted your condition instantaneously to me."

"Ah, so we've been rescued, and not."

"Yes. I can be here but I cannot move you anywhere, to your home planet, for example. But a star ship due to arrive here in about two of your years can transport you home, at a much faster rate than your space sail ship. But you have another option. You may spend as many years as you want on this planet, carry on with your explorations, and, after some intensive instruction from me, explore other worlds throughout our galaxy. Then, you can bi-locate back to your Earth and pass on these breakthrough discoveries to your fellow beings there. Or, at the end of your decided length of stay on this planet, a star ship can transport you home with all your new knowledge."

Silence fell as each pondered in their hearts the meaning of this encounter, and all they could gain for themselves and for the whole Earth. So vast and moving the moment proved that Aashi felt hot tears stream down her cheeks.

Planet Uphill

After the initial thrill of the *Star Wing* crew's alien encounter, hard work became the order of the day. For Bretori began to instruct them on the elementary principles of bi-location. But these principles presupposed an advanced degree of Kworthi psychology and science, difficult subjects. Once mastered, they would be ready for core stuff. So, immersed in this torturous learning, mental gears ground away until they near smoked. By the end of each daylong session, the crew needed big chunks of sleep.

Waking up one morning, Captain Grieg informed Dan and Aashi of an upcoming mission, their first. Honored and terrified at the same time, there they sat in the captain's private chamber. Captain Grieg, aided by electronic charts, first showed them the constellation Cassiopeia. Specifically, their target would be the planet HR-8832, at 21.35 light years from Earth. This star, smaller and older than Earth's, formed the core of a lively solar system of seven planets, two of these super-sized Earths, one like Jupiter, the others with natures unknown. To one of these mystery planets, the 4th from the sun, they would be sent, via techniques they had supposedly mastered.

Sometime later, tense but expectant, the pair of brave explorers prepared to set out. Put through the transit sequence, everything flowed smoothly. Then they opened their eyes and looked around. Under a starry night sky, they stood on the slope of a mountain. Checking their instruments, the atmosphere read breathable, temperature mild. The gravity tug feeling lighter, they concluded the planet not dense. But here the first contradiction hit. For if this planet small and not dense, why the enormous mountain whose slope they stood on? For it rose up before them so high its peak faded from sight.

"You thinking what I'm thinking?" Dan spoke, breaking the silence.

"If you mean this massive mountain not fitting into the other parameters of this planet, that's a yes, Dan. I never expected this, numbers not adding up right from the start. Mmm, and this mountain slope so steep…ah, but look straight up. I see faint light above, like dawn in the works?"

"Now that would be a welcome sight, even though the stars here shine brightly, partly illuminating this slope for us."

"Ah yes, you're correct on that, Dan – they do light our way to a point."

"Yeah, a little, anyway. Ha. So you know what, Aashi? Looks like we're destined to climb this K2 x 10, just to get a sight of dawn from its far off peak."

"How long do you suppose it will take us?"

"Well, with the gravity here fairly light, our going should be good, although the trek long. But first, let's poke about right here for signs of life. Ah, wait, look, right below us! Looks like some kind of plant."

Stirred into explorer mode, they examined the plant.

"Aw, no way!" Dan exclaimed. "A plant with tiny square leaves?"

"Ha, yes, correct again, Dan. Do you suppose they have square roots as well?"

"Aw come on, Aashi, no high school humor, please. I mean, just think about it, a plant with perfectly square leaves. Look, look closely – perfectly shaped! Just what on earth could it mean?"

"That we're not on Earth anymore, or haven't been for years now. Oh, but I get what you mean, Dan. It's not a natural shape for a living thing…a living thing that we know of, at least."

"What possible evolutionary advantage could this provide the plant?"

"Mmm, yes, what advantage? Ah, if the insects here are round, perhaps the square leaves confuse them. So they look for food elsewhere."

"Okay, look, Aashi, we're not going to get anywhere if we don't stay serious."

"Well anyway, life of a sort exists here. I'll take a sample we can analyze later."

"Right. And then we start our climb."

And so they did just that, wondering what they would see beyond the peak. But then, as they climbed far up the slope the peak remained as high and elusive as ever. This unexpected phenomenon began to rattle them greatly. Dan also became aware that dawn now seemed stuck on the brink of day.

"Okay, Aashi, time to reassess here. By now you've noticed it too, we're not making progress."

"Do you think it an optical trick, Dan? Could a quality of the atmosphere bend shapes in some weird way, creating illusions? While we actually approach the summit?"

"An intriguing possibility, Aashi…the whole place doesn't seem to make sense in an optical way…ah, but that's a thought trap we'd best avoid. Because if we're dealing with optical tricks, there's no point in continuing our mission. Then again, something in my gut says to push on, that in the end this place will make sense."

"Alright, Dan. Let's not give up on this planet. Possibly our mountain alone causes this baffling effect. Ah, wait, perhaps we should descend it into more rational lowlands? Just to see what happens?"

"Rational lowlands…ha, yeah, nice thought, that. Yeah, let's see what happens."

And so they began to descend, but after just one step froze in their tracks.

"What the…? Can't be, just can't be…"

27 • Worlds Beyond the Cloud

"Oh, but it is, Dan, we're climbing again, only this time up a slope pointed in the opposite direction."

"Or the same slope switched around in some trick way?"

"No, not the same slope, Dan. Look at the stars. Positions have changed."

"You're right, Aashi, star positions have shifted, but sunrise still approaches."

"Or sunset? That would explain the change in star positions."

"But maybe we stand on a new slope, sun still rising, and so we view a different field of the night sky...hmm, still, maybe you're right, Aashi. Maybe the sun *is* going down now. On the other hand, it could be the same slope switched around, since we haven't changed our position on it, not in any rational way, at least. Aw man, this place – just not making sense! Well, there's one thing for sure: we don't want to hike into night on this gonzo planet...if in fact the sun now sets. Aw crap, let's turn around and climb again up the initial slope, back into a theoretical sunrise, at least."

"Yes, I agree, Dan, better dawn than sunset, even a dawn without birds. Oh, but wait, I just had an insight. Let's walk up three paces, turn left, walk three more paces, descend three paces, walk three paces right, and lastly re-ascend three paces again."

"Oh great, the one thing we didn't pack, Aashi, anti-flip out pills."

"Yes, I know, it sounds like nonsense. But just humor me, Dan."

"Okaaay. But this place just gets more bizarre by the minute."

And so, at the conclusion of this maneuver, there the two stood at the top of their massive mountain.

"Alright, okay, would you care to explain *that* one to me, Aashi?"

"Oh, it was just a wild hunch, Dan. But since it somehow worked out, I can now state with some confidence that we're not on a mountain at all, but rather some kind of pyramid. You see, Dan, the height of the Great Pyramid on Earth is 5773.502692 inches, the inverse of the square root of 3. So, its dimensions match the object we stand on here, us being somehow reduced in size, odd as that sounds. As for how the ritual we just performed factors in, well, allow me a moment to think about it."

"Gonna take more than a minute to think *that* one through, my love. This whole scenario – sounds like you were the ghostwriter for *Alice in Wonderland.* More clearly now I see that we've landed ourselves into some kind of absurdist situation. The universe is rational, this we know. So where are we now? In some kind of hell? But no, there's still some weird kind of logic here."

"And beauty as well, Dan. Just look at that!"

And so Dan did, what he saw smooth grey rock twice his height, with an A shaped base and slender left leaning upper part, boulder atop. The boulder, perfectly round, ever so slightly rolled first one way then another, remaining balanced.

"Naw, can't be a natural wonder, or can it?"

"Perhaps it could be, Dan. Oh, but then again, it looks like some kind of stone sculpture. May nature make art?"

"Well, indirectly yes, and the principles of everything else. But I see what you mean, Aashi. Could fit into some kind of gallery back on Earth."

"Oh no! What about *that*?" Aashi exclaimed while pointing. For to their left now a ladder appeared, perfectly straight, rung after rung ascending till fading from sight.

"Aw crap, that's gotta be the limit! A ladder rising from the top of a purported pyramid, ascending non-stop into space…with maybe no end at all, just rung after rung after rung, infinity rising. And you know, to technically finish our climb, we'd have to ascend that ladder as well...man oh man, does my brain need a rest!"

"Wake up, Dan, wake up! You're spinning around like a cotton candy twirler, making a mess of our bed."

"What? Cotton candy twirler? Just what the heck's going on here?"

"You tell me, Dan. First you jabber away in your sleep, sounding upset, and then you go vestibular on me."

"Vestibular? Aw come on, Aashi, gimme a break. Just tell me. Aw no, wait a minute. It was all a *dream*, only a dream, but one helluva dream, let me tell ya."

"What happened in your dream?"

"Well, first of all, Captain Grieg had–"

"Dan! Rise and shine, ya lazy slug. The both of you – report to my briefing chamber, 0800 sharp," the captain snapped as he walked by.

So there sat Aashi and Dan at 0800, both looking perplexed. Captain Grieg taking note, his scowl only deepened.

"Okay, Dan, out with it. Your expression looks damn near acidic. What's the issue?"

"Oh, nothing, Captain, nothing at all. Just a double whammy of a dream, is all."

"Ah hell, what timing – that movie set mind of yours acting up, right before you're about to get an important update. Wait. This is a job for Doctor Solander, our physician and shrink."

"Aw come on, Captain Grieg, no need for me to deal with his shrink half. "I'm good to go, whatever you have in mind."

The Captain ignoring Dan's protest, soon the doctor arrived. Cajoling Dan into telling the dream, at the end of the yarn the doctor just smiled.

"Ah yes, a common enough malady, Dan, and how well I recall it myself. Ya see, kid, for the last several months we've all been busting our butts to learn a new body of knowledge. Yeah, and so it's prompted me, for one, to reflect on my over ten years of studying space medicine, and other related dense subjects. Felt like walking uphill all the time, no end in sight. Never thought I'd make it to the top, and if I actually did, I'd drop dead from exhaustion."

"Ah yeah, now I get it. Jamming so much info into my head that skull seams dang near cracked. It's been uphill, for sure, lots more in store, from what Bretori says."

"That's true, Dan," the captain cut in, "we have lots more to do. But um, I'm curious now. How would you best sum up your traumatic dream?"

"I would sum it up, Captain Grieg, by quoting Heraclitus: The way up and the way down is one and the same."

"Ak! Not the Zen paradox angle again."

"Ah, yes, I get it, Dan!" Aashi piped in. "Think about it for a minute, Captain Grieg…ah, and think of the common expression – something or someone going downhill."

"I've felt that way for years now."

"Why?"

"Because, Aashi, my life only seems to be getting tougher as time goes by. So, one could well conclude that the reason is there's less of me and more of things to do. Anyhow, it's all part of a human life cycle, a natural curve."

"Au contraire, Captain Grieg. You, of all people, should know a curve is a bent line. So let me suggest to you here that as far as a life cycle goes, that curve bends up. In other words, not only are you *not* going downhill, but the path in front of you has gotten even steeper. Conclusion: there's no such thing as going downhill in life. That steep slope we encounter in time just causes us more strain. But in the end we push on, ever striving for high ground."

"Ha, striving for the high ground…is that why some people like to climb mountains as high as possible? Are they cheap thrill seekers by nature?"

"No, nothing of the sort…because, Captain Grieg, people who push themselves to the limit up high mountain slopes also do it for a less obvious reason than thrill seeking."

"The less obvious reason being?"

"Well, let me put it this way: every single person born carries a stone block with them, stowed away in a backpack."

"Start making sense, Aashi, or you're Doctor Solander's next customer."

"Oh now, think about it, Captain Grieg, before speaking again."

Quietly the captain pondered this image.

"Alright, okay, so we all carry a load in a way…but why a stone block?"

"Well, the stone block is a metaphor for our given task in life. Think of an oyster making a pearl, the time it takes and energy, but the pearl sums up the efforts of the oyster's life. So the stone block we carry with us equals one more block to add to the pyramid of life. Yes, and we all aid in its construction, with awareness or not. So, like those struggling laborers of old who erected those pyramids block by block, every human being does the same with their destined task. Small or large, we each have a block to drop off at the end of our climb – our humble contribution to the good of the whole."

"Huh, the good of the whole…been listening to Dan too much, Aashi. Ah, but wait. Large or small these blocks, you say? Then here's my take on the matter: Dan will drop off his block through a donut hole if he doesn't get on the ball, and I mean right quick."

Diamond Head

With First Mate Dan Stafford still shaking off his baffling dream, Captain Grieg informed him that in fact he and Boatswain Aashi Stafford had been chosen for their first exploratory foray using Bretori's bi-location technique. When the captain further informed him that the star HR-8832 would be their goal, he was taken aback.

"How can this be? That star, the star in my dream! The dream I just told you and Dr. Solander about. Next you'll be telling me our ultimate goal that star's 4th planet! How do we explain such an inexplicable thing? I mean, I had no knowledge whatsoever of this upcoming mission."

"Look, Dan, your dream story doesn't mean shit now. So don't turn this briefing into one of your baffle-gag sleight of hand card tricks, okay? And by the way, this mission was alluded to at our last general meeting. Thought you were pretty funny, eh? Sitting in the back with fake paper eyes stuck to your eyelids as you snoozed away."

"Did you really do that, Dan?" Aashi asked, disbelieving.

"Aw come on, guys, just something I saw in an old movie and just had to try."

"I'd fire you, Dan, but your bus fare home would bust us. So just tell me now: are you up to this mission or not?"

"I'm up to it, Captain Grieg."

And so, prepped and ready to roll, after the requisite sequence, there stood Dan and Aashi, on the 4th planet from the star HR-8822. Yet no baffling wonders greeted them now. First they noted that the sun gave off reddish light, an eerie effect. Next aware of standing on a sandy white beach glowing orange, they noted a vast clear sea, breakers sounding. Atmosphere checking out okay and temperature safe, anchoring their minds in this new place they took initial readings. The sea to their east turned out to be freshwater. Turning west, a shrub dotted plain stretched out, with an anomalous pointed hill some 200 meters from the beach. On the horizon way off, rugged mountains rose. Then in the sky overhead, several flying creatures appeared, looking much like birds but lacking feathers.

After an hour of probing about, these seemingly small discoveries proved mentally draining. They did, after all, inhabit a wholly new world. And so they felt entitled to sit on the beach for an impression sharing session.

"Well, Dan, our mystery planet is sure not the nonsensical one in your dream. Oh, but it's still a strange experience. Mm, because in a way, this planet looks vaguely familiar – sea, beach, large birds of a sort, and yet my feeling can't be described. "I'm in a new world…on the other side of all that we know, a shadow land with sunshine."

"Ah yeah, Aashi, something like that. Feels strange to me, too. I mean, this planet, at least the spot we sit on, appears Earth-like in a way…although the reddish sunlight gives it an alien aura. Still, overall it feels familiar, like a watery Mars with primitive plants of some kind? Plus more gravity. Oh, but something tells me all is not as our surface impressions perceive them. Something under the skin here, I feel it. Ah, Aashi, look! But don't move too much. I think we're about to witness a true life adventure."

And so a scene unfolded. Out of the sea three creatures emerged, one behind the other. Dan perceived them newt-like though larger, about the size of cats, with wet shiny skin, gill-like structures, and tapering tails. With small undeveloped limbs, they swished their way up to dry sand, pushing for the land beyond the beach. At this point one of those reptile-like birds called out. Four more appeared, eyed the waddling creatures, and then swooped to conquer. But then the newt-like creatures did an odd thing. Two of them began to alter their course, flattened bodies now looking larger. The third creature contracted its body, so looking smaller. Then doubling its speed, it made for higher ground and the cover of brush. His comrades though, moving too slow, became a meal for the rep-hawks, Aashi's word for the reptile-like birds.

"Well," Dan said when it over, "nothing like a familiar sight, creature eating creature, usually the slow ones. Ha! So in nature, Aashi, you must be able to split in haste or you become a lickity."

"Oh, very funny, Dan. But you know, in a sense that scene equaled one creature completing another the hard way."

"True, but if those sea creatures could think, I doubt they'd conceive being eaten in such measured terms. That third one sure wanted to make it, and did. One wonders what's in store for it. Hmm, and what would it seek on dry land? Maybe it wants to lay eggs?"

"Ah yes, Dan, like sea turtles needing dry land to lay eggs...but turtles need soft sand to dig in. Our creature will find only rocky land above the beach."

"Yeah, but lacking shells and smaller than sea turtles, right away our guys were waddling meals, like fresh hatched baby turtles scrambling for the cover of waves."

"Right. So here's what we have to do next, Dan: sit tight and wait to see if our third creature returns to the beach and darts for the safety of water."

"How safe would it be in that sea, do you think?"

"Good question, but one step at a time."

As luck would have it, about three hours later, oh so cautiously the third creature reemerged onto the beach. And just as fast as a waddling newtling can go, it made for the water. All too predictably though, five more rep-hawks appeared. And so they swooped to conquer, but the ratio here wrong. Five of them and one newt equaled a sharp squawky fight. Three soon flapping off, two still feisty rep-hawks nailed the newt right as it reached the water.

"There we go again. Creature meets creature to meat up."

"And Darwin lights up a cigar. Ah, but wait, Dan. Think of our newly adopted home planet, Proxima Centauri b. How did that planet evolve an ecosystem predator free? How odd that our first planet would be such an anomaly."

"Yeah, odd at that. But now we stand on more familiar terrain. What we just witnessed is what our science would predict for extraterrestrial life, a food chain like Earth's. Yeah, a creature has to be fast or it becomes food. Anyway, time to analyze the scene."

"Yes. Ah, and about this sea: our instrument will tell us much. We should get those readings before sunset."

And so that evening Dan and Aashi poured over the day's gathered data. Amazingly, the sea data suggested that the creatures lacked predators there. Baffled by this anomaly, they tried to come up with an analogy from things they knew.

"Ah yes! Dan, I recall a bit of datum that may help us piece this all together. Think of the axolotl, those strange newts of Mexico City back on Earth."

"Axolotls? What the heck are they?"

"Huh, a surprising missing tile from the first floor of life science knowledge."

"Ho boy, talk about your irritating verbal snip fits. Just fill me in, okay?"

"Axolotls are amphibians, newts, to be precise, newts that can turn into salamanders. Oh, but that transformation depends on how safe they feel. You see, Dan, axolotls will remain immature newts in the water if too many hungry predators pad about on land. Ah yes, and the Aztec had a legend about these creatures. The story goes that some axolotls choose to remain in water and never morph into adults as a type of, um, adolescent rebellion, one could say."

"Would the Aztec put it that way?"

"No, but they did say that by staying in water axolotls chose to remain stuck in youth, never to grow up and grow old. This thought may sound appealing to some, but not to the Aztec. For them, to be deprived of growing into maturity and ultimately dying would rob we humans of our proper destiny, ascent into the divine."

"An obscure but intriguing bit of info, Aashi. But how does it help us in the here and now on this alien planet?"

"Well, for one thing, Dan, consider our seaborne newtlings: they too appear to feel more secure in the water, where oddly enough they have no predators. For another thing, like axolotls, in the sea they mostly eat plants, according to our data. I would further guess that their bodies would morph before transitioning to full time land dwellers, something like newt to salamander."

"Huh, yeah, some interesting points. Ah, but now, could this be some unusual kind of divided planet, herbivores in the sea, carnivores on land?"

"Mm, a novel thought, Dan…but the answer is unknown at this point."

"You know, Aashi, this could be a long study. So we should probe about for several more days, maybe longer. Yeah, 'cause I'd hate to break off this study with no conclusive findings whatsoever."

"I agree, Dan. We need more data before returning to Proxima Centauri b."

And so the study continued, uneventful for the next three days. But then, again the explorers witnessed another newtling foray to land. This time seven tried, with two finding cover. In time the two creatures returned, both darting for water. Again the rep-hawks appeared. But as one newtling flattened and turned in circles, drawing more predator looks, the second one made it to water. That evening Dan and Aashi discussed the day's findings.

"So what did we witness here today, Aashi? The most logical assumption that this episode represents a recurring event – the struggle, the death, the eventual triumph of at least one of these creatures."

"I agree, Dan. Still, at this point in time we can't close the door to other possible interpretations."

"Are you suggesting, Aashi, that today's little drama a first time event? That only *now* has one of those creatures succeeded in making it back to the sea?"

"Oh, yes, I know, Dan...quite a far-fetched notion. But we can't just rule it out. Still, based on our sparse data so far, other possibilities abound."

"Yeah, lots of doors wide open yet. Could take chunks of time to fathom. Ah, but do you see the weak link in the chain of events of our study? In other words, we have no idea what motivates these creatures to strike out for land."

"And yet, Dan, to have disturbed them as they scrambled inland would have muddied the study. We simply can't interfere at this point, only watch and wait."

"Yeah, true enough...aha! But with our winner newtling back at sea, we can follow its inland trail, at least, to discover its goal."

"Tomorrow's mission then: find that goal!"

And so next morning, before tracking the newtling's path inland, the explorers first took readings from the sea. Wide-eyed, Aashi could scarcely believe what she read.

"Dan, our newtlings grew overnight! I can measure the difference. How can this be?"

"Huh, yeah," Dan agreed while noting the readings, "what might this mean?"

"Something unique is unfolding here. I say we put off the inland mission, try to figure out what goes on at sea."

"Yeah, maybe the sea is the crux of the issue."

"What do you think our sea's most defining feature so far, Dan?"

"Well, for one thing, since we understand now this planet has one large hot core heating its mantel and crust, this fairly warm sea water would act to speed up growth…while keeping the air temp on the mild side, too."

"True, Dan, but why would that growth acceleration start just now? And that right after our survivor made it back into water?"

"Okay, here's the plan: you stay here to probe the sea, I trek inland, find out where our winner newt went. We need all the clues we can find here right away."

"Right. Good luck, Dan."

Off Dan went to the point where their newtling had made it to land. Instrument finding its trail, Dan followed it to that odd shaped rocky hillock. Then he saw it: a small cave opening up. Excited, light in hand he crawled in and poked about. In about forty minutes Dan pieced together, at least in part, what had occurred in the cave. Excited, out he popped to return to the beach and Aashi.

"Aashi! Look, look what I found!"

"What is it, Dan? Oh my, it looks like some kind of raw diamond?"

"You got it, Aashi. Anyway, our newtling entered a cave where these gems can be found. So, our winner must be a female."

"What? Why would you say something like that?"

"Oh, you know that old joke – diamonds are a girl's best friend."

"Oh right, so I marry a poor scientist like you…mm, but thanks for the diamond, Dan. Perhaps we can cut and buff it back on Proxima Centauri b, work it into a pendant or ring."

"Ha! See what I mean? Anyway, this is so baffling. No food in that cave, no other creature inside for a tryst, just these rough diamonds. Oh, but wait. My readings showed a trace of that creature's blood."

"Anything else?"

"No, that's it, unless you've made a discovery in the sea?"

"Only that our creatures continue to grow, nothing else...but I'll keep trying, take some 3-D pics we can look at tonight as we try to piece this together."

That night, during a brainstorming session, Aashi noted something of interest in one of her pictures.

"Dan, look! Look at this creature! Look closely at its head and tell me what you see."

"Let's see...well, it looks like some kind of abnormal growth?"

"But Dan, look closer as I enlarge and enhance."

"Ah yeah, now I see it...that creature has a rock in its head, small and transparent."

"A diamond, Dan, a diamond! Somehow, our creature worked that diamond into its head in that cave! Remember the blood?"

"Oh man, so bizarre! Why? What on earth would that creature have to gain by lodging a gem in its head? And now this inexplicable growth spurt..."

"Diamond Head! Our creature's new name."

And so it went all day, as the explorers took new readings and strove for an explanation. None came that day or in the ten which followed. What did come though were dozens of newly enlarged and physically transformed diamond newts, as Aashi renamed them. Not exactly fearsome in appearance, their size and energy alone drove off the rep-hawks, these new ones no easy pickings. Successive landings followed, until it became clear to them that they witnessed a pivotal moment in this planet's odd evolution. For by all appearances, these four limbed creatures with small tails and long necks looked like the crew taking over dry land, at least in these dampish parts.

They noted as well that the skin of these creatures thicker, making them more sun resistant.

So now, the pair had to struggle anew with how they defined intelligent behavior. For on the one hand, an instinct appeared to have acted to prompt the diamond hunt. On the other hand, with the object of the hunt so esoteric, they were forced to reconsider how instinct and thought interact. With all this newness churning away, like a bolt from the blue a fresh thought struck Dan.

"Aw no…Aashi, something unique occurred to me."

"But Dan, just about everything here is unique."

"True, but this is a singularity of a thought. Consider this: we know how stars have internal irregularities that cause them to vibrate. Vibrate, yeah, in rhythmic patterns some have called star songs."

"Oh, Dan, I see where you're heading here, on a path so untrod…"

"Right, breaking some kind of new ground here, pretty damn exciting. So anyway, we further know that these star sound waves, this music, can't be transmitted through the vacuum of space. Ah, but these rhythmic star vibrations cause corresponding flickers in starlight…"

"The light transmitting the patterns the sound waves contain."

"Right. So then, what would be a good medium for picking up those light variations? Well, consider a diamond. Our precocious Diamond Head, using an instinct so complex that it intersects with thought, outfits itself with new head gear, head gear which transmits these light signals into its brain. Recall how we have observed our hero newt swimming so close to the surface, head above water. Then, perception of the star song causes powerful new excitation, prompting a growth spurt."

"And our hero Diamond Head, in turn, transmits these light altered brainwaves to his comrades, in some way yet unknown…"

"Right again. So they all begin to grow and morph, become what they were meant to be all along but had been thwarted, in part, at least, by carnivorous land creatures."

"Which they banish with their new powers...oh, Dan, it's starting to sound something like Proxima Centauri b, where non-predators form a self-sustaining ecosystem."

"Yeah, something like that, in a smaller way. So, Aashi, we're confronted here with the possibility that non-carnivore dominated planets might not be rare, that the X factor here appears to be planet bound biological life linking up with greater cosmic forces from beyond...somehow transmitted, in part, at least, by certain cosmic vibrations, star songs a part of the picture."

"Mmm, yes, and what a picture emerges here, us so far off in space and on our own! And Bretori...like a wise teacher, wants us to learn all this newness on our own."

"Yeah, and wow, so many new associations are hooking up in my mind...just think, Aashi, our Earth, with its obvious bitter life struggle...with so many believing that struggle promotes the appearance of traits which aid in a species' survival...which makes sense in that context, at least, the stronger crushing the weak. But we have to consider the possibility that our own evolution could be one-sided, lacking the vital connects we seem to be witnessing here and on Proxima Centauri b as well. Ha, but this planet...such an enigma. Just imagine, carnivores pushed aside by plant eaters...at least in this instance. And what an odd overall situation here...an older star with a planet apparently at a formative stage of evolution...where does this type of evolution lead, do you think?"

"Yes, Dan, how fascinating to discover where this sequence ends. Oh, but even with the precise nature of life on this planet still open to interpretation, we do have one rock solid fact: we've witnessed a bold reaching out on the part of creatures we now must conceive of as not limited to a self-enclosed biological system. No, but rather, intimate connections exist, binding them now to cosmic evolution as a whole. So these creatures have an inborn drive to make the partial more complete, their diamond hunt crucial. And perhaps we could conclude that life as a whole shares this drive."

"Huh. Should we jam diamonds into our foreheads, do you think?"

"Naw. Just make me a beautiful ring with the diamond you fetched."

The Two Worlds

The crew of the *Star Wing* on Proxima Centauri b continued exploring their world. As for bi-location and deep space exploration, Dan and Aashi, having the requisite traits, were tasked with that project. But when Captain Grieg suggested Dan venture to the galaxy's core, Dan wondered why. So the captain related the image he'd had of a night sky blazing bright, and how like a tide it rose up in his thoughts. Now, conventional wisdom held that life would not thrive there, tightly compacted stars causing harsh radiation. Even so, he argued, better to check out a few planets there, unique as they would be.

With this thought in mind, a twin star system in the constellation Sagittarius was chosen, one with an Earth-sized planet. Now, this planet orbited fairly far out from its binary suns. Yet with two energy sources, this fairly distant planet would be warm. And so the explorers set out, hoping for luck.

"Here we are again, Dan!" Aashi exclaimed while looking about, "on a whole new world, and a lush looking one! Just look around us, a garden, almost, so luxuriant the plant life here."

"Yeah, safe air to breathe and hey, it's on the hot side...but natural enough, since two suns rise and set here."

So knowing now the planet safe they fully materialized. Next they began to take readings as eyes roved over the land. What they saw reminded Dan of the Amazonian Rainforest. For like that noted basin, tall trees formed a canopy here. And, while the vegetation unfamiliar, the moist air, scents, and bird-like creature chatter matched a template within. This helped to make them feel at home, to a point. But with thunder and darkening clouds overhead, they scrambled for cover. Under an outcropping of rock in the midst of this lushness, they found a snug enclave.

"Mmm, on the romantic side, isn't it, Dan?" Aashi smiled, "snuggling in a sheltered nook in some mysterious jungle as pounding rain falls."

"Romantic? Sure, yeah, but we need to stay on our toes here, Aashi. 'Cause ya know, I'm rapidly getting the sense this a meat-eating planet...and we don't want to end up a couple McNugget for some jungle hunter."

"Right. And now that you mention it, Dan, I do sense something padding about..."

"Yeah, and even though we've a weapon this time, I'd rather not test it on whatever slinks about out there."

"Let's set up our bubble tent on top of this rock. That should make for safety."

"Good idea. Hmm, but what about this damn rock, anyway? So out of place with the scene here."

"Not so out of place, Dan. About 150 kilometers west of here I'm detecting an enormous mountain."

"Aw no! Not like in my dream, I hope."

"No, this is a real mountain, Dan, rising right out of the jungle."

"Ah yeah...a whole range like the Andes?"

"No, Dan. This mountain rises up a singularity of rock in a lush jungle basin...a range of mountains possibly off in the distance...oh, and yes, a river I detect as well."

"Anything else?"

"Yes, our intuition registers in real time as well, a large creature nearby...ah, and farther off a patterned creature cluster of some kind...maybe a humanoid settlement? From here, that's what my reading suggests."

"Wow. Right off the bat this place teems with life and excitement, but danger as well. Ah, what about the day length here, Aashi?"

"Approximately thirty hours, Dan, with sunset eight hours off."

"Well, in spite of the slinker about, let's explore a bit after setting up a safe camp above on the rock. We're armed, after all, and we need to take a close look at this plant growth."

"I agree, Dan, we need to poke about before calling it a day. Oh, and then at night we'll get to see that super luminous night sky, the mere thought of which has captured Captain Grieg's imagination."

"Yeah, should be quite the sight."

Yet with the coming of night, the sky failed to wow them. In fact, to Dan's mind at least, the night sky here looked not much brighter than Earth's. Next morning though, they beheld a rare sight. For as their new world's twin suns arose, they filled them to the brim with purest wonder. For one thing, two suns in the sky at once cast a hard to describe spell on the land. For another, that slow motion cosmic dance seemingly made their thoughts oscillate. Possibly then, those two separate gravity engines, waves of power between them, had a real effect on their minds. But then, while caught up in this moment, Aashi had a new thought.

"Ah, Dan, perhaps a clue to our dimmer than expected night sky relates to the moistness of a rainforest, where fungus abounds."

"Dunno about that, Aashi. With the densely packed stars in this region, that effect of fungus would be minimal, not enough to explain the night sky's lack of brightness."

"True, Dan, on the face of it. But keep in mind we're on a new world, the nature of life here of necessity different. So, airborne fungus here might have evolved in a way that made a filtering effect more possible. And my instruments show fungus quite dense here."

"Ah yeah, an unusual thought….a high concentration of fungus, so concentrated it dims the night sky, like a living dust cloud…and that on top of humid air…but we can't draw conclusions just yet."

"I agree, Dan. This will take some study."

"Yes indeed, plenty to study here. Aha! But wait, after we probe the various angles at this location, we should make for that patterned creature cluster to see if humanoids live here. Ah, and then, via our language translator, we may be able to converse with one."

"...and learn the cultural lore of this place! Great idea, Dan. A people's culture naturally reflects much of the world which birthed it."

"Right. Well, let's pack up and get going."

And so they did, on a trail they found which led towards the creature cluster. When they spotted a young woman by a stream washing clothes, they knew their data base about to quadruple. So, in order to make that contact smooth, Dan suggested Aashi alone approach their subject, she of gentle speech and charming presence.

With grace and tact, Aashi approached the young woman, both hands forward and open, smile on her face. Looking up with a start as Aashi drew near, the young woman, brown skinned with long wavy hair, in simple attire and clean overall, stood poised on the brink of several reactions. Taking note of this, with slow easy movements, Aashi bent down on her knees. "Hello," she said, "my name is Aashi. I have come from a distant land. Can you help me find my way through your beautiful forest?"

A moment of silence ensued. The young woman's eyes roved over the stranger, lastly to rest on her eyes. Then, liking what she saw, she smiled a bit.

"My name is...Kar-solta. I live in the village nearby, the village of Ayit."

"Ah, yes, we felt the presence of others. You must wonder what brings me...and a companion yet down the trail...to your land."

At the mention of another alien presence, the young woman tensed up, but just for a moment, as Aashi's smile melted her fears.

"Yes, yes, I *do* wonder, with all my might, what brings so, so…"

"So strange a woman to your land?"

"Yes, so strange, like no other woman I have ever seen…and dressed so oddly."

"What brings us to your land is an, um, a quest for new knowledge, new knowledge of other places, creatures, and especially intelligent beings such as you."

The young woman smiled at being addressed in this way, sensing to a portentous event in the making.

"What is a, a quest?"

"A quest is a search for some desired thing. For example, pretend you have never been in this lush green forest. You have a bundle of clothes that needs to be washed, but you know not where a stream is. So you search and search and ah! At last you catch sight of this sparkling stream."

"Ah yes, I understand!" She laughed. "And so you sought me!"

"Yes, yes we did. We want to learn of your people, how you live, and what your highest hopes are."

"Highest hopes," Kar-solta echoed, looking down then up again. "Well, the way you said your question…it makes me think of Shining Mountain."

"Shining Mountain…a beautiful name. Mountains, yes, mountains are important to my people as well. How they pierce the sky and affect us so."

"Ah, yes, it is the same for my people, too. How that mountain affects us…"

"And fills your dreams?"

"Yes! Yes! And fills our dreams."

At this point, Dan concluded that Aashi had made a new friend. Would be hard not to like her, he thought with a smile. And so, after several more minutes of engaging conversation, Kar-solta invited Aashi and her companion to

Ayit. Graciously Aashi accepted, Dan presenting himself just then with one more calming smile.

Arriving at the village, they caused a ripple effect. For the villagers, struck by Kar-solta's alien friends, hardly knew how to react. But then, placing her hand on Aashi's shoulder and telling the people all she'd said, the ripples smoothed out and lovely reflections appeared. Cautiously they approached Aashi, a bold few touching her silky black hair, children inspecting her hands. Dan they more cautiously assayed, and yet in the end felt assured that Kar-solta spoke the truth. At this point, a man more colorfully dressed than his fellows stepped forward. The village leader, he introduced himself. Next he asked his guests several questions. Satisfied with their answers, he informed them they were welcome, and that his people would assist them in their quest for knowledge. He further informed them that a special meal in the evening would be served in their honor.

And so a festive occasion arose out of nowhere that night. After a rich spicy meal, the village leader, or Burthune, as the people called him, entertained his guests with tales revealing the lore and hopes of his people. These hopes went far back in time, to a time when disease ran rampant throughout the land. But then, with the arrival of strange visitors, a new order emerged. These visitors, making Shining Mountain their base, taught the Gresharté, as they called themselves, how to obtain better lives. And so, settled on the mountainside, the Gresharté made much progress. In time they discovered a way to stop the disease that claimed many lives. They also taught the people how to make useful compounds and tools. But now, the Gresharté on the mountain were quite distinct from their rainforest brethren, keeping more to themselves than in the past. Still, once in a while they descended their mountain to deliver a message or tool.

Concluding this part of his tale, the Burthune moved on to stories of topical interest, successful hunts, dangerous storms, and visits from afar. Still, he noted, no visitor here had been as starkly foreign as Dan and Aashi, reminding him, he said drawing close, of a long ago encounter with the Bretanards, the people whose arrival had changed their lives. At this point Dan and Aashi could practically feel eyes alighted upon them, the people breathless and waiting, for what the couple knew not.

So then, after a pleasant stay of ten days, Dan and Aashi prepared to set out for Shining Mountain. The Burthune had arranged transportation upriver by boat. He warned them though, that visitors from below were no longer allowed on the mountain without the mountain dwellers' consent. So with the explorers packed and ready to go, Kar-solta approached. Touching again Aashi's shoulder as she often now did, they could see how sad she was to see them leave.

"Oh, Kar-solta, don't be sad," Aashi said, placing her hand on the hand on her shoulder. "We will return to your village before we depart, and even after we leave will come back in time, I promise. Really now, how could it be otherwise, with you our new and special friend?"

"It is well, then." She smiled. "Oh, but before you go, one thing remains to be said."

"Oh? And what might that be?"

"Um, well, our Burthune spoke of our people in the light of our highest hopes, as is natural for a leader...but not of our secret fears."

"What causes your people to fear, Kar-solta?"

"We fear, we fear not ever finding fulfillment for the yearning within us."

"Fulfillment of what, Kar-solta?"

"Something which has always stirred us, like wind through leaves...and, like wind, we scarcely know of its nature, only that it calls to us."

"And so you hope to fulfill this invisible longing…ah, and how precious to all beings fulfillment is, most especially our kind."

"Our kind?"

"Yes, Kar-solta, *our* kind. We are more alike than different, you know."

"Yes, yes, you are so right, Aashi. I feel this now in my heart to be true. We share common dreams and hopes…and yet, over time a dream alone loses its power to sustain a man or woman."

"Yes, I understand, Kar-solta."

"No, you do not understand all of what I say, Aashi, because, because your appearance has stirred our dreams in light-filled ways. And now you are leaving…"

"Kar-solta, you must believe what I just said. We will come back again. Don't you trust me?"

"In so short a time, you have become like a sister to me, Aashi. Yes, I trust you."

Here she hugged them both and swiftly departed. Aashi, turning from Dan, brushed a tear off her cheek – and then they were off for their boat.

The trip upriver proved an eventful one, causing extensive note taking. But when at last they caught sight of that towering sacred mountain, instantly the big picture hit home. Cone shaped and snow-capped, a perfect mountain icon it appeared, so much more affecting with the creative force it embodied than anything else in the land.

"Clearly volcanic," Dan said, after pulling his eyes off the sight.

"I would think by the look of it," Aashi agreed, "although it could well be extinct…or at least I would hope so, with a considerable number of people living on it."

"Huh, yeah…ah, but look at the way it forks that wrack of clouds colliding with it halfway up…mm, yeah, what a sight and a symbol, a mountain like this…"

"Yes, Dan, an unforgettable sight. Um, but do you think its people have forgotten about their no unauthorized climb rule?"

"Only one way to find out, Aashi."

With that defiant remark, soon Dan and Aashi found their way through thick forest below the mountain, getting drenched in the process by off and on cloudbursts. By the end of the day though, a determined effort put them on an upward trail. So there they spent a wet night snug and dry in their clear bubble tent. But soon they wished it had a dark color as lightning lit up a wet wilderness four hours from dawn. Still, highly charged and dramatic, it posed no real danger.

They set out on the upward trail at dawn. With this focused effort, by noon they had climbed through the clouds. Onward they trudged, through a forest one would expect at higher altitude, trees similar to pine and spruce. Into mists again, they wondered at the lack of a challenging presence. But then, showing through the mists now, a high wall blocked their way. Pausing in wonder, memories stirred of Earth's distant past, when walls like this one common. Beyond that stone block wall, a mountainside sliced in geometric design revealed intricate gardens and Gresharté habitations.

"So what do you suppose we'll find beyond those walls, Aashi? A welcoming host or typically prickly land owners?"

"Your thought supposes, Dan, that we get beyond this wall. You know, I'm beginning to get an odd feel about the types living up here…so esteemed by people with much less wealth. But let's approach the wall and see what happens."

The path they trod led to a gate. To their surprise the gate opened. Looking at each other for a moment, in they stepped, gate closing behind them. Then, two men in robes exited a nearby post house. With no fanfare or explanation, up they walked to the couple to wordlessly assay them. Finally, they nodded to each other.

"My name is Eth-utra," one spoke up. "We do not know who you are but do know that you are...not of our world. For this reason, we allowed you to climb our mountain unhindered. But now, please do tell us something of yourselves."

Pausing, Dan formed his thoughts.

"Yes, we are not of your world, and uh, have travelled here in peace. You see, sir, we are on a quest for new knowledge. So, with this in mind, all we ask is the right to address you with questions which you have the right to answer or not, at your discretion."

"A discreet answer on your part, um, what did you say your name was?"

"Oh, my apologies. My Name is Dan Stafford and this is my wife Aashi Stafford."

"And you are from?"

"Not around here..."

"Your answer borders on rudeness."

"And yet a gracious host first puts tired explorers at ease before conversation."

"You answered well. Please then, allow me to escort you to one of my homes."

Dan and Aashi followed their host, Dan signaling Aashi for caution. At length they reached a two story stone house. The grounds, well kept, had trimmed trees and flowerbeds of artistic design. Inside, high ceilings created a spacious effect, windows placed just so allowing beams of light to slice through the chamber. Up the stairs they were led to a room facing out from the mountain, complete with a plant lined balcony.

"Is this room to your liking?" Eth-utra asked.

Admiring the polished stone floor and array of shapely plants, Dan turned to his host.

"A beautiful room–"

"–with a view," Aashi added, smiling.

"I am happy it meets with your approval. You may rest here before refreshments are served downstairs."

With that, their host and his associate departed.

"Well, Aashi," Dan began, while sitting on the bed to test its softness, "this is some turn of events."

"Do you think it's a risky shift, Dan? I read your signal for quiet. Oh, and do you think it's safe to talk freely in our new room?"

"Yes, Aashi, we can talk freely…my gut tells me at least, that plus the fact that out on the balcony no one will hear us."

Moving to the balcony, they closed the glass door behind them.

"I know, Aashi, I know, maybe I'm being overly cautious. But this kind of response is built into our species, with its long history of conflict and betrayal."

"I understand, Dan. But think for a minute. We truly hold the high cards here, to use an old expression. We know more of them than they know of us. We also know, if not beyond the shadow of a doubt, at least to a strong degree, that these people are not hostile. Think of our friend in the village, Kar-solta."

"Yes, Kar-solta…and that whole village, in fact…not aggressive people by nature, and the people here of the same stock. Only the externals differ. So yes, I think we're safe, but still, you know, the onus is on our host to first tell us something of himself and his people before asking us similar questions. So, if that's how he and others here conduct themselves, then so much the better."

"Right. Let's see what happens next."

And so they rejoined their host in the spacious main chamber below. Food and beverages served, Eth-utra relaxed.

"Allow me to first tell you of my people and *our* quest, as you express it. Yes, so, to begin, having talked to my kind below in their lush rainforest, you already understand shades of our heritage. Oh, but the story full told will fill you with wonder. As you already know, our planet, Ad Platia, is located near the center of our galaxy. And as you undoubtedly know, this fact means that our high concentration of stars makes for harmful emissions of radiation. In the past, my people suffered because of this, a deadly disease causing cellular growth to malfunction."

"We call that illness cancer."

"Then you know the dangers of this disease. So, with these harmful emissions coming from densely packed stars, our people faced this disease on a large scale. But then, again in a mist obscured past, a people arrived from beyond our world, the Bretanards they called themselves. They too had a quest, as you say, to help peoples they encountered. And so they established this mountain colony for us, staying for a time as teachers. They shared and taught us much of their advanced science. With their advanced knowledge, they showed us how to alter the living structures of the airborne fungus which becloud much of our warm and moist planet."

"To what end?"

"To make this airborne fungus capable of filtering out harmful emissions coming from stars in our night sky. These emissions, as you know, are what set off this disease. So, once this great task was accomplished, this sickness almost ceased for my people."

"Quite an achievement. But what about this mountain? Its upper parts high above this blanket of moist air and mold? Are you not exposed up here to those emissions?"

"No, we are not overly exposed. If you look with care tonight, you will see a small moon overhead, in geosynchronous orbit."

"What? A moon in geosynchronous orbit? We've never heard of such a thing."

"The Bretanards brought this about. Our one small moon in the past had orbited our planet. But this clever people made it stand still over our mountain. Under this moon, a protective cone is created below it as radiation from the stars deflects off its surface. This means that our night sky has a reduced level of these harmful emissions. Secured by this clever arrangement, we are free to continue our work of expanding their knowledge."

"A noble pursuit. Your people should be proud," Aashi said. "But um, perhaps an unintended result of this, meaning your separate lives on Shining Mountain, was to alienate you from the rest of your kind? It is, um, clear to us, as outsiders, that your manner of life and interaction has become much different than for your kind as a whole."

This simple observation caught Eth-utra off guard.

"I uh, well, yes, our styles of life do differ, but so too our environments. Surely you must realize how environment molds a people, to a remarkable degree."

"True enough, environment has impact on us. Still, the wall…was it necessary?"

"Well, there are jungle hunters, you know…dangerous animals, the world below no kindly one. And, to carry out our work, we need ah, not only this security but a measure of solitude, too. As scientists you must know this."

Dan and Aashi both reflected a moment.

"True enough, Eth-utra, true enough," Dan spoke up. "But now, might something else factor into this social equation? We get it now that the fungus you genetically engineered protects the people below from harmful night sky emissions. And obviously your genetic engineering insured that the fungus itself poses no risk to your people. But um, to be perfectly honest, I get the sense that other things enter the picture here."

"Yes, many other things. Did you expect to learn them all in one sitting?"

"No no, you're right. Foolish of me. But now, let me just say at this point that Aashi and I come from a planet far from our galaxy's center. Our development was one rocky road, let me tell you, impacted by harmful forces of nature and various conflicts of our own making...which we overcame, to a point. And so our visit here – to further develop our better instincts, or 'the better angels of our nature,' as one of our leaders once put it."

"Then you come to other worlds to better yourselves, acting out of self-interest?"

"Oh, but the fruit of our enrichment flows downhill, in a manner of speaking, to enrich other peoples."

"Peoples downhill...lower than yourselves, you mean?"

"No, that's not what I mean! We only try our best. That's all we can do."

"It sounds as if your people struggle yet."

"Of course we struggle yet! We are no gods. Are you?"

"So, well, if you are so far from being perfect, how can you criticize us? We seek the same good goals as we see them, to perfect our lives."

"Ah, and there's the rub, my friend, as our kind would express it. Not all agree on what a higher being, or more plainly speaking, what a human being is. More than a few in our 20th century thought this goal of perfection could be reached by exterminating other races."

"And so a people like you is going to enlighten us?"

"Only you can do that," Aashi cut in.

"What I think here," Dan picked up the cue, "is that Aashi and I need a bit of time to digest this conversation. Brief as it was, we must all realize that as beings from different regions in our galaxy meeting for the first time – well, just a handful of ideas exchanged, so highly charged with new content and context, is mentally taxing, at least for us."

"Yes, yes, your proposal is sound. Let me suggest that for the rest of our day you tour the gardens on my grounds, absorb this new environment, match the knowns to your own. This will relax you and prompt clearer thinking."

And so the explorers did just that. Outside now, breathing more freely and drinking in green, their minds felt refreshed. But, while sitting by a mini-pond with trickling waterfall and a ring of miniature trees, this peaceful bubble was popped by Eth-utra's silent associate.

"Forgive me if I startled you. Would you prefer that I left you in peace?"

"No no, that's quite alright," the gracious Aashi answered. "Please, feel free to sit with us and share your thoughts."

"Very well," he replied, seating himself. "My name is Sal-noah. I have worked in the inner circles of our government for twenty years. But to spare you a very long story, allow me to speak my mind freely."

"Please do speak freely."

"Yes, the core of my tale is just this: we, as you explained of your own people, struggle still with our own imperfect natures. Oh, but make no mistake, we can and do think clearly and accomplish much. But…as is natural with beings of our imperfect nature, we, we sometimes, oh, how to express this…"

"You sometimes lose sight of the big picture?" Aashi suggested.

"Yes! Yes, exactly what I wanted to say, because the as yet unspoken truth here concerning my people is that we have discovered a means of upgrading the genetically modified fungus which shields the lands below from radiation."

"Really?" Dan said sitting up. "Can you speak of it now?"

"Yes. So yes, we have produced a new strain of fungus that would, if released in our atmosphere, at the same time protect the people below from radiation while allowing more night sky light to shine down on them."

"So your people below could hear the star songs deciphered from twinkling starlight?" Aashi cut in.

"Oh, so amazing! You know of the star songs, too?"

"A recent discovery of ours."

"Then you know that a mind can decipher the oscillating flickers of a sun into rhythmic sound patterns…"

"…which can prompt marvelous new developments in a mind so infused. Yes, we do. But what you say now…distant stars have this same effect?"

"In our galactic region, yes, so compacted the stars here. So yes, the twinkling of stars can be read in a similar way, supposing a mind equipped for this endeavor."

"I see. And how is a mind here equipped to do so?"

"It is quite a simple concept, really. We wear jeweled crowns at night, receptors below each gem, transmitting information into the brain. But we need wealth and isolation to live in this way. Our people below in the forest provide us with food and labor too as needed. We pay them small amounts of money in return. Some of this they send to their poor families."

"A system we have known on Earth," Aashi noted.

"But not all on our mountain favor this system. I and others too, want to change the way we live. We desire to introduce this new strain of fungus into our atmosphere, allow our kindred below to thrive in our starlight…oh, but we would need to invent a new way of accessing this process to make it less expensive."

"An age-old problem on our Earth, regarding not only the fine things in life, but food and water as well, at least in times past," Dan responded, sighing.

"Oh," Sal-noah went on, "and let me tell you a secret. Yes, by mentally reading the rhythmic patterns of a single or double sun, this star song process results. But – a night sky full of blazing stars, once read in the mind, registers as a chorus, this chorus having a multidimensional effect on the mind…the difference overwhelms at first. We have learned to tap into these rhythms in careful degrees."

"So, let me see if I understand correctly. You belong to a faction that would end this system of separation and allow the average person to benefit from this star process…"

"Yes, that is correct."

"But it appears to me the hard part is getting this new strain of fungus released in the air – my assumption here this new strain designed to replace the current strain."

"Again an accurate assumption."

"But the hard part…"

"Would involve um, a break in, a crime of sorts, in order to steal the vials containing this fungus. Oh, but this would be a daunting feat, at best, impossible at worst, the lab in question deep inside this mountain."

"Well now, if the existence of this fungus poses such a threat to the established order, why haven't they destroyed it?"

"Because of the Council of Eight, our final authority here. Yes, and so four councillors vote to destroy the fungus, four to preserve it for future consideration. But by law, a majority must vote either to destroy it or deploy it. So the council is deadlocked."

"Huh. An enlightened and yet unenlightened form of government, delicately balanced. What would it take, do you think, Sal-noah, to tip that balance in favor of all people?"

"I, I am uncertain how to answer your question. Are you saying that our council is the route of attack for us, and not a covert action?"

"Well, a covert action could work. But the problem there, Sal-noah, is that about half the people on your mountain would feel defrauded by such an action, robbed of the precious expression of their voices via your council. I'm assuming here your people more or less evenly divided on this issue, correct?"

"Yes, again your assumption is correct. And the people chose our councillors."

"Ah, well now, what do you think the prospects are that both Aashi and me, or one of us alone, could address your council?"

"Ah yes, a good question, your arrival here momentous in ways…quite possibly they would desire to hear you address them as to the nature of your quest. They would be most curious to learn of it."

Just then, out of the blue Aashi stirred.

"Dan, something just occurred to me. I must leave at once, return to the village of Ayit."

"What? Why, Aashi, why?"

"Soon you will know. But can you arrange to meet with the Council of Eight?"

"Easier said than done, Aashi. But then again, I think I can do it."

"Oh, and I apologize to you, Sal-noah, for my hasty departure. Rest assured, time will answer the question etched in your face."

And so Dan did in fact arrange a rare audience, after speaking with Eth-utra on the matter. In seven days Dan would stand before the Council of Eight, explaining their mission objectives. And, just as Sal-noah had noted, realizing the weight of this event, the council viewed it as a way to deepen their own knowledge, as well as share some of their own. The contentious issue of their two-tiered social structure was not on the agenda, as far as they knew. In the meantime, Dan was free to explore Eth-utra's spacious grounds as well as nearby parks for all the people. In so many ways, he could see this was a near perfect order. And, if not for the fact that he knew how most people lived here, at least on this part of the planet, he would have viewed it as a model worthy of emulation by other peoples. But then again, he thought, the more basic life of the rainforest dwellers had an appeal of its own, the pulse of nature coursing through the people's daily lives. In many ways their lives had found fulfillment, and yet a vital spark missing.

Soon the 7th day arrived. Dan, embarrassed at having been caught primping in front of a mirror, with a mutter and blush allowed Eth-utra and Sal-noah to escort him to the seat of their society's government. The structure impressive, large and made of polished white stone, it had an air of the ancient, yet intersecting lines suggested abstract thought.

Inside, chambers rose up high into vaulted ceilings, not unlike Earth's cathedrals. Like them too, beams of light passed through these high arched chambers, contrasting with cool shadows. The Council of Eight chamber, on the other hand, had a more intimate feel. After all, only eight people were highlighted here, with a small gallery of other representatives witnessing proceedings.

So there stood Dan, feeling small and alone, in front of the council. Intimidating it felt, until the Prime Councillor addressed him in cordial tones, inviting him to freely have his say. And so he began his brief address, outlining the origin and purpose of his mission on their planet. He even drew smiles when he mentioned how their Captain Grieg had longed to see the brilliant stars of their region up close for himself. Thoughtful reflection he drew as well with his frank admission of Earth's less than stellar history, replete with wars and social upheavals. But then he drew wonder and respect when he pointed out the heights his people had reached by overcoming their own self-centered natures. Just then though and out of the blue, it appeared, into the chamber walked Aashi with Kar-solta, and how they contrasted. For Aashi, in prim modern dress and only neck length hair, looked worlds apart from Kar-solta, with her lovely long hair and plain rainforest attire. But Aashi had insisted she not adopt mountain dress for this occasion, convincing her the simplicity and grace of her people's attire had a rare beauty.

To the surprise of all, next Aashi put forward Kar-solta to speak before her. Blushing, looking down at first, as if ashamed of her humble origins, she next raised her eyes and beheld the Council of Eight one by one, gazing into their eyes. This had an uncomfortable effect on some, an engaging effect on others. For this type of visit would never have been allowed had not Aashi politely but firmly explained that the council needed to hear Kar-solta's story, now an intimate part of her own. Reluctantly, and without precedent to guide them, they had allowed her to enter the most august chamber in their small nation.

So there she stood with upraised eyes, poised to tell her story. Now the councillors knew of their lives and customs – from a distance. Yet the face to face effect, all felt, would strike them vastly different. This proved to be the case as Kar-solta presented the best of her people's achievements. Moving on to her own life, she shared with them impressions of her youth. But pausing she looked down again, as if unsure how to proceed. Then, finding her muse, she looked at the panel to sum up her feelings.

"And last of all, let me tell you of my arrival here just last night. Oh, I must confess that my friend Aashi here had to take my hand and guide me to our quarters for the night. Why? Well, because I could not take my eyes off the night sky, a sky never before seen by most of my people. What a banner of glory it is, triumphant splendor, creation as it blossoms like an enormous swirling flower of light. Just to drink in this vision, so marvelous a vision, why, I could almost hear music, as odd as that sounds…yes, music in the light of a million stars…ah, and I could see them throb away, almost as if the heavens have a heartbeat…yes, mountain high and stars alive somehow speak of the deepest hopes of my people. Oh, and thank you all for kindly allowing me to enter your mountain domain, and to stand in your noble presence."

Having listened carefully, the Council of Eight had a faraway look in their eyes. How they had come to take for granted the gift in the heavens above they scarcely now noticed, merely tapping the energized songs to nurture their minds. And yet this rainforest dweller, prevented by the fungus from experiencing this for herself, in many ways had more polished thoughts than their own. How much more so would she shine if she fully heard the star songs, they had to wonder.

Taking his cue at this point, Dan, with Sal-noah by his side, sprang the secret meaning of their meeting. With studied words he begged the council to vote once again on the issue of the genetically altered fungus. Dan told them as well what Kar-solta had told them of long cherished dreams eventually fading away for want of fulfillment. Most of the council reacted with care, yet one man sprouted a scowl.

"Dan Stafford of Earth, you have expressed yourself well. And yet, when the story is full told, you speak in ignorance. For surely you know, and that from your own planet's history, that a civilization, like a living structure, has a division of function by needful design. Clearly you must see that in order for us to continue our research and intellectual expansion, we need certain others to serve our lower needs so we can further these higher ends, of course for the good of all."

Realizing at once that no other words would sway this council member, Dan strove for a way to disassemble the rigid man's logic.

"Ah, well, esteemed councillor, in my defense, allow me to say just this: the point of a pyramid is shaped by all blocks comprising its structure. In fact, the convergence defined by the base defines the point in space the tip is aimed at. And so we may conclude, blocks at the top merely act to focus and point, the real force at work here defined by the base."

"A rather empty concept, I must point out," the councillor mocked.

"Oh, but Councillor, the concept of *spacious* could, in a negative sense, be defined as empty, in a positive sense, lack of encumbrance."

Hearing this, the councillor pretended he hadn't. Yet seeing one more opening, Dan again spoke up.

"Kar-solta and her people dream of joining a new Gresharté consensus, in all respects. Will you let her down? Will you thwart the fulfillment of her whole being?"

This last thought had impact, deriving its punch from Kar-solta's singular presence. So then, Dan's proposal was adopted and the councillors voted – this time six in favor, two opposed. Solemn yet happy beyond compare, the three friends left the chamber. That night they met on the balcony to rehash their triumph. Instead, giddily they looked above at a spangled swirl oozing light. Yet Dan and Aashi in the end preferred that sky's reflection in Kar-solta's eyes.

"I knew you were our special friends," she said with a smile, hand on Aashi's shoulder. "You, you have brought this wonder about for my people."

"No, Kar-solta, *you* made it happen," Dan countered, "you made it happen by speaking clear words of truth to that isolated council. You made it happen."

"But I was so awkward, my words blurting out…"

"You were yourself, Kar-solta, and that proved more than enough to do the trick. And before you say another word, we're going to commemorate this occasion with a toast."

"A toast?"

"Yes, we call it a toast, and Sal-noah provided the wine, or something like it. Ah, but what really matters is not the drink but the action and sharing of mood. This special mood then lodges in memory. Don't ask me how."

Pouring three glasses of wine, Dan raised his, Kar-solta and Aashi likewise.

"To a friendship that will always bear fruit."

"To friendship," Kar-solta concurred, as three glasses clinked.

The Edge of Time

Just before departing to their next selected planet, Dan squeezed several thoughts into a flutter of time. First he wondered why Captain Grieg had chosen such an anomaly for their next mission, arguing against his decision. For one thing, a planet with zero axis rotation and no seasonal tilting would be an unlikely place for advanced life to have evolved. Then too, while this planet orbited its sun counter-clockwise as does Earth, with orbital speed unbelievably slow, in effect this 1/3 Earth-sized planet did not move in space. Captain Grieg had countered that this near total lack of movement greatly intrigued him, it being impossible according to science. The passage of time on this world could prove an enigma worth probing, he'd insisted. Last of all he'd said its small molten core proved this distant planet still alive in a sense.

"Time to see who's right!" Dan said, as he and Aashi felt air. Then, the planet showing signs of plant life, they fully materialized. Almost immediately, Aashi swept her instrument about, looking for higher life forms.

"Captain Grieg has finessed you again, Dan," Aashi beamed warmly. "We have indications of possible humanoid life somewhat beyond the horizon."

"Huh. Whose side are you on, Aashi? Smiling like that at our crank of a captain's one upping of me."

"Oh Dan, really. Sometimes I wonder about your level of maturity. I smile now at feasting my eyes on a life bearing planet. Take a good look around."

As Dan tuned into the sight, his annoyance abated. Yes, what sheer joy for eyes to greet a lively sphere, companion of an unnamed star on the galaxy's opposite side. Next he considered its raw distance out in space from the sun. And yet of course the sun's enormous size compensating for distance, the planet's surface proved warm. So as Dan's brow smoothed and wonder increased, he gazed out on a desert-like scene, not unlike some on Earth, rocky and bare to a point, yet harboring life.

"And now we inhabit this planet as well," Aashi smiled.

"Yeah, not a bad deal," Dan smiled back. "Hey, wait a minute. The feeling of this place…as it seeps in, gives me a sense of, ah, a sense of something not here?"

"Mm, something not here…yes, Dan, I feel something lacking here too, some essential something, besides lack of motion…still, you know, the plant life about us is real enough and sunlight abounds."

"Oh yeah, lots of light and a fair amount of plant life, deserty looking brush…or maybe shrubs?"

"Ah, Dan, look closer," Aashi said while kneeling down. "They resemble more little trees…shapely trunks and branches, complete with tiny waxen hot weather leaves."

"Right, and dwarf trees could well result from an arid climate…oh, but would that not presuppose a full-fledged version?"

"Yes and no, Dan. On Earth it would be so, but not necessarily on an alien world. Still, we should keep that in mind."

"Yeah, we should. Aha, and look at the way these small trees, or shrubs, or whatever, all show a windblown effect in the position and shape of their branches."

"Ah yes, correct, Dan, almost a cultivated bonsai effect…quite attractive."

"Wait a minute," Dan answered, standing erect and looking about, "something not right here, something not adding up…"

"What's not adding up?"

"Dunno, Aashi. Give me a minute or two to poke about, size up the situation."

Dan walked about 100 yards north of Aashi's position while carefully scanning about.

"Aashi, what's our position on this planet anyway?" he loudly asked.

"Let me check…oh, how intriguing. It appears we landed on the exact center-point of the sun-ward face of this planet," she answered as Dan returned. "Odd that we should land right here by sheer chance. But tell me, Dan, exactly what did you notice to prompt such a question?"

"Wait. Give me another moment or two."

So Dan walked off 100 yards south of Aashi's position, scanned about and returned.

"Well, my love, we have yet another cosmic mystery on our hands here. It's like this, Aashi…ah, wait. Just pivot around in a circle and tell me what you notice."

Aashi did just that while carefully scanning.

"Oh!" she gasped, "Correct again, Dan. These shapely little trees were not sculpted that way by the wind. Their supposedly wind shaped sides all point towards where we stand, as if this center-point has some positive attracting kind of force."

"You got it, Aashi. And so our first unanswered question concerning a planet near stationary in space, as Captain Grieg said, a theoretically impossible state. Why would this come about, do you think? Some kind of screwball gravitational effect we just don't know of yet?"

"Possibly, Dan, but then again…"

"Right. Possibly not."

"At this point, Dan, we need to evaluate what's going on in this one particular spot. We should make it our camp for the night, at least, and on the following day as well."

"Gotcha, Aashi, got your message by default. This new situation's not gonna fully sink in all at once, we so conditioned by a 24 hour cycle. Yeah, this place, this place with no night and maybe no real day?"

"Oh, come on, Dan! I'm not going to let you get away with *that* one without some kind of explanation. Ha. No real day…"

"Well heck, just from a psychological perspective I think it makes some sense. Think about it for a minute: how do we grasp the meaning of day if not through its absence, night? Not to mention a dark stormy night."

"That's all you got on this one, Dan? Just one straight pitch?"

"Huh, well, just a bit of curve to the ball here, Aashi. Think again. Right off the bat we got an unreal feeling about this planet, besides the standing still sun, like it ah, like it lacks some kind of essential something…something more than a psychological effect. So the question is, can essentially freezing movement in space bring about real, concrete changes with a planet's hidden dynamics?"

"Mm, yes, Dan, it does have a surreal feeling to it, this stationary world we've stumbled into…psychologically speaking, the effect has power, for sure…as for lacking some *measurable* essence, an essence which makes a world a true world, well, that surely is no given…would take time and effort to prove."

"Right. Maybe a good point to begin our study with. And we have to deal with one layer of this planet's weirdness at a time. So let's go over the basics here first: in a sense, the planet we inhabit now is at a virtual standstill, an almost stationary ball in space. Just think about it, Aashi, zero rotation, a counter-clockwise orbit so slow as to be imperceptible…would take a hundred years for an inhabitant here to notice any change in the stellar arrangement. Can't be many planets like this in the entire universe, and one supporting higher lifeforms, no less."

"Yes, Dan, according to my initial readings, some ways beyond the horizon. But this spot, we need to study this unique spot before any lateral ventures into this strange new world."

"Agreed. Let's set up camp and see what develops."

And so they did. Once settled in, they set about examining soil, plants, and insect-like lifeforms. The hours melted away but of course not the sun, locked firmly into place, set at high noon. At first they found this welcome as it made for a highly visible exposure of their objects of study. But at about the customary hour for dinner, as they ate and talked a sense of unease developed. So after eating they continued with their studies, something they had never done before, rather reserving the evenings for themselves. At the customary time for sleep, they entered their dark tinted tent. Dan managed to doze off, but soon woke up, Aashi missing. With a touch of alarm he left the tent, scanning for her. There she sat on a rock, gazing about in the noonday sun, as if she saw something special. Silently walking up, Dan heard her talk to herself, something she had never done before. Startled when Dan put his hand on her shoulder, turning, she smiled.

"Oh hi, Dan! What are you doing here? I thought you were out on some far-off planet doing a study."

"What the heck you talking about, Aashi? You okay?"

"Don't fret," Aashi said as she turned left, as if to speak to someone else, "he's always like this when he's lost in thought...exactly like when we first met."

Here Aashi laughed, as if responding to laughter.

"Aashi, I think that ah, I think..."

But before Dan could finish his sentence, he noticed palm trees on his right, complete with a sparkling white beach and clear sea beyond. "Dang, honey, that is one knockout of a bathing suit ya got on there...really brings out the um, the tropical island side of your nature, with emphasis on tropical. Now I could say lots more there, sugar pie, but hey, words just don't do ya justice..."

"Huh. Just who are you sweet talking, Dan?" the indignant Aashi on his left piped in as she swung him around by his shoulders. "And why did you try that crude ploy to pull my attention away from a chat with old friends?"

But before Dan turned away from the crank who had plucked him from a dream scene with Aashi, hitting like a thunderbolt, a real thought seeped in. Taking the Aashi on his left by the shoulders, he gently but firmly shook her.

"Aashi, Aashi, snap out of it! We're awake and asleep at the same time, dreams seeping into daylight. Must have something to do with being in this ultra-rarity of a spot."

Confused at first, Aashi then grasped the gist of what Dan said.

"Oh, yes, as you say, Dan, ultra-rarity making for ultra-weirdness. Oh, but the dream images…they keep popping up, drawing me back into them."

"Okay, look, we can't stay here, Aashi. Studying this phenomenon up close just isn't gonna work. Let's break camp and head out, pronto. Hopefully in several hours we might be on firmer psychological ground."

And so with concerted effort, Dan and Aashi briskly walked due east of their center-point landing site. In fact they cheated a bit by using the airlift feature of their boots. In this way and in several hours, dream images started to fade out as conscious thoughts triumphed. At this point taking a break, they sat in the shade of a large rock, first looking across a stark flat land and then at each other.

"Well, Aashi, we sure enough wrapped that study up fast! Even so, what a bundle of impressions we now have to process."

"I agree, Dan, we certainly have a full plate to deal with here. But no instrument of ours will ever come up with a reading for what we just went through. Just too alien, too far removed from all established norms. Still, we may at least work through our impressions and propose some possible explanations."

"Yeah, but it's gonna sound more like sci-fi than science, Aashi. Just don't know where to begin here...ah, but first, we have the mystery of materializing exactly on that center-point. Can't be gravity that drew us there, but something sure did, some unknown principle or force..."

"I agree, Dan, no accident plopped us down there, that one particular spot...ha, I think here of your comment to Captain Grieg about an invisible line running from this planet to its sun, center-points involved here."

"Yeaaah, but I don't see how that image alone does us much good...I mean, if the sun here were non-rotating like this gonzo planet, then something like that might fit...but this sun rotates at a rapid rate for its size, 35 hour clockwise cycle at its equator, this planet having zero spin."

"Right. Ah, but wait, Dan. Try this idea on for size. First, since there's no up or down in space, imagine we view a solar system chart, one which places the sun and planets on a horizontal line."

"Okay. Now what?"

"Now rotate that chart's horizontal line to the vertical position. So here, now we have the sun at the bottom, planet above."

"Very artsy, Aashi. Do continue."

"Now imagine, if you will, that clockwise spinning sun sending out an imaginary rotational spiral, successive waves of that spiral getting farther apart as they head out into deep space."

"So what comes next?"

"Next, picture this planet's western hemisphere interfacing with those incoming spiral waves. Now, so far, Dan, this scenario would apply to any normal planet, given its sun's clockwise rotation. But a normal planet has far greater velocity than this one. So it would zip right through these spiral waves, them closing behind the planet's opposite side. Ah, but the slow slow almost no motion state here, what does that suggest regarding such a dynamic?"

"It implies that the side of the planet pointed away from your spiral waves would have an, um, a wake by default, created by the planet's blockage of your proposed spiral wave flow. Ah, but no ordinary wake, this wake would behave the opposite of how a normal wake would. It would be static...ha, Zen paradox here."

"Correct, Dan. And this paradoxically static wake would not expand as an ordinary wake would. About the same width it would remain, in my estimation. Ah, but now the crucial point. Both edges of this wake would comprise a boundary between what within the static wake and what beyond. And what would be within this static wake? Well, just space, yet space in some kind of ratified state, unperturbed, for one thing, by my proposed rotational waves. This calming effect might even be intensified inside this wake to the point where it somehow resists other types of space movement, solar particles, for one, a wind in space, in a sense."

"Um, but Aashi, these spiral waves of yours, while making for a nice picture, are ah, to put it a bit bluntly, an imaginary construct of your mind."

"Huh. Stephen Hawking once said there could be as many universes as perceptive minds are capable of conceiving."

"Yeah, but that's just one of the expansive statements one would expect from a great man. Ah, and also a way of being modest, you know, like saying his conception's not as special as his supporters back then believed them to be. I mean, if I said our moon back home was made of green cheese, would that make it so?"

"Are you saying my idea is just as outlandish?"

"Um, no, actually not, Aashi, your idea having a certain hawkingesque feel to it. Aw heck, so tell me more about your new theory."

"Okay. So next, think of what Einstein said about time equalling movement through space. And space itself moves with particle flows and its continuing Big Bang expansion. But the boundaries of this rare planet's wake...so strange these zones would be, conceivably causing a disruption in the flow of space-time itself?"

"Quite the extravagant picture you paint here, Aashi, but at the end of the day we still have to view your idea as imaginary in its familiar context, not a possible cosmic one."

"But it got you thinking, did it not?"

"Yeah, that it did, and it got my own mental gears turning, too. Ah, but maybe the dream pole effect lingers on in us yet."

"Oh yes, a possibility, Dan, but it need not be a wholly negative possibility, now need it?"

"True, it could go either way, benefit or hindrance. So let's keep this in mind."

"Yes, let's do that, Dan. Ah, wait, one more point. The dawn zone band across this planet's western hemisphere would mark the midpoint of this unraveling spiral interaction, running through the center of our planet's western hemisphere...aha! And the exact hemispheric center-point of this line would also mark the equatorial center-point! the location we would reach if we proceeded straight east across the dusk band and then through this planet's night side...the point we would emerge to. Don't you find that a fascinating thought, Dan?"

"Um, kina...but the significance of all it escapes me at the moment, my love."

"Well, as you just suggested, let's file it away with other impressions for now, Dan."

"Right. And I think it safe to say we're in for more wonky workings here, especially if we find intelligent life."

"Yes, just what kind of minds would this near stationary world produce? And will our language translator work with them?"

"Time will tell, my love. In the meantime, we should keep heading east, our intermediate goal the twilight band on this planet. Ah, and what a singular sight to behold that will be."

"Yes, Dan, a singular sight."

Digesting their first enigma, next day Dan and Aashi proceeded eastward. The flatlands now mixing with rocky hills, they noted their unmoving shadows with some sense of wonder. In fact, they stopped on the crest of a bluff just to watch for a while, thinking now of the shadow on a sundial back on Earth – time, simple time, captured by the movement of the sun and ever shifting shadows. Dan thought then of a story in the Bible where God had granted extended life to King Hezekiah, this gift represented by the shadow on a sundial going back ten degrees. Then he thought of Stephen Hawking's concept that in a slowly contracting universe, time would flow backwards. But the great man later changed his mind and said time would still proceed forward, but too late to erase the notion of memories in the future.

Then too, even if no shadows changed in this world, them moving neither forward or backward, time went on. They could not stay here, never to grow old and die. Somehow the laws of the universe would override the appearance of no time progression. But that could be partly explained by the fact that the laws of the world of their birth upheld their being. That could not change for them...or at least Dan did not think so. Still, looking at the static shadows again, how compelling the illusion appeared.

A few more days into their journey east, Dan and Aashi came across a clear bubbling spring, a welcome sight on this fairly dry planet. Inching towards dinnertime, they decided to camp there. So, by pools of calm water surrounded on two sides by rocky bluffs, they took their ease. By now they had more or less recovered from their unusual experience at the planet's sunny side center-point. Even so, a dreamy mood for the couple lingered on. In this mood, Dan sat alone by the water, recalling how as a child water had captivated him so. Then he poked a stick into the water and took note of its refraction. It appeared to bend up in the water, giving the stick a slight v shape. But now, the simple fact that light bends when entering water somehow struck a new chord. With an inhalation and skyward look, Dan waded back to the bank, sat down and thought, remaining in that posture for twenty minutes.

"What is it, Dan? Are you okay?" Aashi asked, putting a hand on his shoulder. "You've been sitting there like a bump on a log for a while now."

"Ah, have a seat, Aashi, have a seat. Time for me to share a little insight. No wait, a double insight now. Let me start with the most recent. So okay, we're still in a bit of a dreamy state from that spot's effect, but you know, sometimes that's okay. I've read how inspired moments in not just art but science too happen when subconscious and conscious minds merge, to a point."

"Ow, how exciting, Dan! A Picasso moment."

"Picasso or Pissaro? I always mix those two up. Anyway, maybe insight number one is no insight at all, with me just recalling things we've both read or heard. Ah yeah, like an art lecture at school I didn't sleep through. Seems that Renaissance artists said, as far as painting concerned, that the center is relative to its point of observation. Ring any bells?"

"Oh, yes, Einstein said that about the universe."

"Indeed he did. And you know, art is kind of a dreamy type thing, subconscious images playing a large part in authentic production. Ha, and Einstein thought in images too…so the dream thing for us could go either way, muddling our thoughts or raising new possibilities. But now, insight number two is, um…"

"You can't recall it now?"

"Only that the v shape refraction gave to my stick suggested to me that, um, aw crap, suggested something to do with geometry and space…"

"That's it? A geometric connection?"

"Yeah, guess so…plus alignment kinds of things…maybe the meaning will come back to me later. In the meantime, all this thinking has made me hungry. Too bad there's no trout in these pools, just silvery little things…ah, but now, we've only seen small creatures so far, correct?"

"Ah yes, correct, Dan, and a good observation at that. Yes, only small creatures so far…interesting…oh, but let's eat then think some more."

And so they did, and as a customary Earth dusk did not materialize, curious, they poked about the pool for a while. At this distance from the center-point, the sun appeared in about a one o'clock position. Shadows somewhat deeper then, Aashi took note of the bluff across the pool. A slate grey stone with a touch of sheen, she imagined how it might make attractive building blocks. But then, near one of the many fissures she saw it, or thought she did: a single tiny man, not much more than two feet high, thin and plainly dressed as he neared the water. But then, feeling Aashi's eyes alight, almost like a swish of wind it disappeared into a bluff crack.

"Dan! Dan! Did you see it?"

"See what?"

"A minuscule man! He, he just disappeared into that crevice, right there, by the bank of the pool."

"Ah oh, the negative side of the dream effect rears its ugly head."

"No, Dan, no! That tiny man was real, as real as you or me. I know the difference between a dream and a real event."

"Right. Just like the non-existent friends you were yakking with not long ago."

"But they *do* exist, Dan, just not here. Oh, you! Don't you try and sidetrack me now with another subject! We have to investigate that being."

"Well now, does your instrument register a lifeform of that size and nature?"

"Um, no, no it doesn't. But if it found its way into some underground network, well of course I'd get no reading."

Hand in chin Dan sighed, not quite sure what to think. But then he looked once more at the silvery little fish in the water below, slowly lowering himself for an up-close inspection. Noting perfect fish shapes, they didn't look minnowy in nature. Then he thought of the dry country shrubs that looked more like miniature trees. Lastly he looked at the fissure. Yet try as he might, he just couldn't picture a tiny man squeezing in.

"Okay, Aashi, so we'll linger by this pool one day longer, lie low and see what we see. But then we have to strike out east, okay?"

"Fair enough, Dan. But I know what I saw."

And so they spent all next day quietly by the pool. Interesting at first, soon it got boring. Still they manned their posts till mission completed, sighting nothing. They then spent one more night, or night cycle for them, by the pool before continuing east.

In not many days they noticed they had entered a trail of some kind, lightly used by appearances, but still in use. But migrating animals of some kind could have made it. Aashi again tried to pick up humanoid readings, failing to do so. They both began to wonder if the first reading from the center-point had been a reliable one. Concerning humanoid life, nothing so far seen confirmed that first reading. But then Dan had a thought.

"What a minute, Aashi. If your initial possible humanoid reading a reliable one, then that grouping would not be far from here, just north a ways."

Aashi aimed her instrument that way.

"Mm, actually, yes, Dan, you're correct. I'm picking up a reading not far north and somewhat ahead of us, proceeding east, a possible cluster of humanoids."

"Proceeding due east, just like us…coincidence, I suppose, but then again could be something here…like an instinct we both share."

"What instinct, Dan?"

"Can't quite put my finger on it yet…ah, but here's the plan, Aashi. We shadow them on their journey east, and then, as we approach the dark side of this planet, we rendezvous with them at the dusk band of this planet."

And so they stayed their course, some kilometers south of a migrating band of humanoids. While this now grabbed most of their attention, they continued probing nature. No startling breakthroughs here, still they had a full plate of impressions to work through. For one thing, they noticed as they moved away from the sun and shadows deepened, plants and animals somehow became more lively. Dan thought about this change and strove for the reason. Could it be something as simple as the sun's increasing angle? For on Earth, of course, the planet's spin through day and night stimulated life, providing it as well with variation. Then too, on Earth as the planet tilted on its axis and brought about seasonal change, lengthening or shrinking shadows resulted. So, on this motionless planet with no seasonal change, maybe the changing angle of the sun alone cued life to react in a livelier way, just as autumn and spring prompt nature to various actions. Could this far off planet once have had seasons? Day and night cycles would provide creatures with the refreshment.

In due time then, when the humanoid band drew nearer to the sunset zone, they had to wonder why this odd migration, and that along the equator. How would such people react when confronted by the boundary of perpetual night? In most cultures Dan knew of, night, while not without a certain allure, overall caused more disquiet than inspiration, especially the long winter nights of northerly countries. He recalled here reading of a scientific study carried out by a man alone up in the Arctic in winter. Six months of darkness he endured, appearing to take it in stride. And yet, leaving his shelter towards winter's end, for just a moment the sun touched the horizon. Nothing surprised this man more than spontaneous tears welling up, along with pangs in his heart. Perhaps it felt a bit like rising from death, Dan had reflected. So, to venture into endless night of their own freewill, these people would have to have a strong motivation. What could it be? Or might they merely camp in that twilight band for a time, perhaps conducting religious rituals? Only time would tell.

Soon the two explorers began to enter the dusk band, and what a rare feeling. For the sun took a long slow set as they pressed onward. Then, as coolness set in, winds began to increase. For here lay a zone where airs mixed, winds from the east cool and moisture bearing. This effect in turn created lively clouds that dumped showers and vanished. But then, moments of calm would return, silence mixing with dim skies.

In time the sun dipped below the horizon. Now, dusk affects most people in quiet ways. But here, as each step forward put you closer to night, the effect was pronounced – a sense of awe and unease plus a curious longing. So, as they stopped for dinner, like an aerial vice, this environment forced a sharing of puzzling impressions.

"So what's the verdict, Aashi? Do you really think we should proceed with our venture? I mean, it would certainly be understandable if you wanted to call it quits.

No telling what kind of alien life might dwell on the dark side...and I'm thinking now the environment itself might also pose a danger."

Aashi paused a moment to digest this thought.

"Alright, Dan. Prudence is part of valor, and perhaps that's what you feel. So let's do this: let's rendezvous with that migrating band. Let's get a sense of those people. Then we decide whether or not to call off our jaunt through the night side."

"Sounds good to me, Aashi. Deal. In the meantime, you know, this could be our last pleasant sleeping spot for a while, complete with fresh spring waters. Ah, and furthermore, I suggest, while we still have some light, an exploration foray after dinner. "'Cause ah, you know..."

"You have a gut feeling about this place, right?"

"You got it."

"What does your gut say this time?"

"Well, this dusk zone...if it feels special to us quite likely too it feels special to the inhabitants here. If so, we don't want to pass over a useful discovery, possibly relating to rites of some kind."

"Alright, Dan...let's have a look see."

And so after dinner, with care they inspected the bluffs by the spring, in time finding a fissure big enough to squeeze into, which Dan did. Light in hand, inward he probed, soon finding a cave. Calling Aashi in, he shined light into the cave and then Aashi saw it: a pictogram of white upon dark rock showing a basic design: a sphere with a cone arising on top, its base merging with the midpoint of the sphere, ending with a taper about four feet up. Stunned, they studied this pictogram, knowing it had meaning they couldn't access.

"Huh, looks like some kind of religious symbol...any guess as to its meaning?"

"Hard to say, Dan, such a simple design...a sphere having deep meaning for many cultures, simply because of the perfection it represents. Ah, but look, look below the sphere. That thin slab of rock...could it be blocking another part of this pictogram?"

Taking a closer look, with effort they lifted and moved the slab, what revealed making them gasp – depicted here an altar, a man splayed out on top, another man standing over his head, knife held aloft.

"Oh man, what the heck is this? It appears, Aashi, that uh, that part of the religion in question involves human sacrifice. Huh, well, they're not alone on that one. But who, who might these people be? Judging from the height this pictogram had been made for viewing, I doubt the small fry you might have spotted made it. And that band of nomads some ways north of us...it strikes me unlikely too that trekking types would have made this...although that possibility can't be dismissed out of hand."

"Which opens the door, Dan, to a possible other type of people living here...cave dwellers who live in the twilight band of this planet and perhaps other places?"

"A hasty conclusion, Aashi, but you just might be right....uh oh...."

"Uh oh what?"

"Yeah, well, if just such a type of folk exists, Aashi, we have two things to consider. First, these proposed cave dwellers might possibly prey on the nomads for um, for volunteers for their rites. 'Cause I'm guessing that nomad types would pause in the twilight band for rites of their own, though likely not involving the ultimate close shave the guy with the upraised knife prepares to administer. Ah, and second, the cave dwelling bit...might it be that by living in caves part time, at least, such types might induce a kind of day/night cycle? Restoring some sense of normality to an otherwise very abnormal situation on this planet?"

"You could be correct on that one, Dan. Oh, but why then would they choose to live in the twilight band rather than a more lit up region?"

83 • Worlds Beyond the Cloud

"Ah yeah, that would suit a day/night cycle better…but this twilight band would be the best place for an ambush, the nomads likely distracted here as they gear up to enter one long night."

"Mm, okay, not an unreasonable premise, Dan. Aha, and if you're right about inducing a day/night cycle, then this factor would appear to indicate a time in the past when this planet behaved in a more conventional way, you know, axis rotation and possibly tilting for seasonal change, to say nothing of a normal orbital pattern."

"Might well be the case, Aashi…oh, but what could possibly explain its complete reversal into such an abnormal planet? A bizarre and extremely rare kind of cosmic disaster? But what, exactly?"

"Mm, such a cosmic flare up is hard to imagine, Dan, and yet our universe abounds with hidden surprises. Wait, a more immediate thought just occurred to me."

"Oh? Let's hear it."

"That um, that this cave might be an extensive one, one just right for cave dwellers to call home…"

"Ah yeah. And if so, we lucked out by entering their domain while they dream of their next big event on the surface…"

"…we fitting the bill nicely for volunteers."

"Right. Time for a hasty exit, Aashi, and I mean double time."

***

Quickly leaving the cave, they decided to strike out north for a few more hours before sleeping. Waking up feeling refreshed and somewhat safe, all at once they tensed up when laughter broke out. Turning about, three men shunted back several children, other young and their mothers watching on in the distance. Dan and Aashi stunned by this scene, another bout of titters calmed them down. One man, appearing the leader, sheathing a dagger strode forward, eyeing the pair. But then, drawing close he smiled and chuckled a bit.

"And just *what* is so funny?" an indignant Aashi asked.

"You, you are funny to look at, both of you. You reminded the children of our comic performers. You, both so odd in appearance and manner of acting, styled just so."

"Styled just so?"

"Yes, your manner of speaking is styled, the flow of your speech like the root pudding our children love to eat...yes, so smooth and sweet."

"Oh, well, in *that* case, my name is Aashi Stafford. And just who might you be?"

"I just might be Olkar of the Dreshi people. No, I am!" he ended laughing.

"Ah yeah, all Dreshied up, but with lots of places to go," Dan added, grinning.

At first looking puzzled, their host next smiled. Olkar stood about five feet high, had a thin drawn face with a well-trimmed beard, desert style robe completing the picture.

"At first we thought you were Zochars and so meant to kill you. But no, how strange your appearance...unique, far away seeming. But your appearance is of no consequence in our law."

"In your law?"

"Yes, our law. Truly you must have laws where you come from?"

"Truly we do, but usually don't bring up the subject when meeting new people."

"Oh, but our law includes events like this, the meeting of peoples. You are now entitled to our hospitality, strangers accorded this treatment by Monesh, our lawgiver. So please, come, join our main party nearby. Then we will share a meal with you. You are also entitled to ask us questions about our origin and customs."

"Thank you very much, Olkar. We look forward to this meeting of minds."

And so, led to a nearby encampment a dozen families appeared, along with their tents. Their mode of dress as well suited the nomad image. As Olkar, they wore a type of robe with head drapes, as seen in hot countries on Earth. And yet no flocks of sheep or goat-like creatures milled about. Rather, Olkar told Dan, his people hunted small game and gathered roots and herbs he said common here. Dan noted how the vegetation here could provide for such a life. For the farther eastward one trekked towards the planet's perpetual night, the greater the rainfall, while still on the dry side. And yet these people's culture appeared more developed than hunter-gatherer types. Could their way of life have been improvised? Had they had a different way of life before? Then too, how did the nature here fit with these people? Quite well, on the one hand, he thought, as their familiarity with nature's ways in these parts rang out loud and clear. And this clear ringing of course, set the rhythm for their cultural lives, whatever its nature. With these impressions and questions then, Olkar had them seated as guests of honor. Simple foods, set before them with bows drew smiling responses. Following dinner, spring water steeped in herbs refreshed the explorers. Then, easing back in folded leg position, Olkar appeared ready to field his guests' curious questions.

"Olkar," Dan began with care, "I wonder now greatly of the origins of your people, the Dreshi. You already mentioned Monesh, your founder…"

"Yes, our founder and savior, too."

"A savior, too?"

Here Olkar exhaled a long breath, clearly pained.

"Yes, our savior. Our story begins many centuries ago. In that distant time, the lives of all peoples in our world were very much different. We had cities, we had grand ideas, sadly mixed with pettiness, but grand ideas still, yes, and the high hopes which went with them...but then, Melzar entered our world."

"Ah, and who was this Melzar?"

"Melzar was, Melzar is, a being of malicious intentions. We soon learned that for Melzar, spreading malice and pain caused him great satisfaction...yes, hard to believe as that may sound to you. For you see, he has great power, power enough to have shaken our whole world."

"So your people were shaken..."

"Yes, our people were shaken, but so too our world of mountains, forests and plains. Our whole wide world shook upon his arrival."

"What happened next?" Aashi asked.

"What happened next was an era of turmoil and confusion. In this era wars erupted, wars such as our people had thought long buried in our past. People fought, you see, for shrinking resources...oh, but now, they also fought out of malice, this malice caught from Melzar's radiating spirit. So, during this time, our population shrank greatly. People began to live in tribes once again, the Dreshi among them, or better to say the ancestors of the Dreshi, for then we had no laws or purpose in life.

Ah, but then Monesh appeared, yes, Monesh appeared, our great seer and giver of law. In this stark and dangerous time, Monesh brought back meaning and order. He taught us two kinds of laws: laws governing daily life and laws which also connect to the whole universe. Of these large laws, he introduced the law of migration. He taught us that in order to feel how the universe itself travels through time, we must travel, too, ever travel, circling our planet throughout our own life cycles. In this way, he taught, we would stay connected to the great universal journey."

"Ah yes," Dan remarked, "the need to connect...so true on multiple levels, small and great...but now, might I ask you an, um, a delicate question, Olkar?"

"Yes. Ask me your question."

"Before this great unhinging of life on your planet...did you have night and day, as in most worlds?"

"*Did* we have night and day?"

"Yes, simple night and day, the sun rising, setting, and rising again."

"Oh, but your question makes no sense to me! Of a certainty we have night and day in our world! How could it be otherwise? Such is the nature of life, is it not?"

Stunned now and at a loss for words, Dan paused for reflection. Brazenly obvious now, a further planetary anomaly had surfaced in its people, or at least in the Dreshi. Best for them not to push on this issue, causing more unneeded turmoil for these survivors of a cosmic disaster.

"Oh," Dan then jumped back on track, "but what of the Zochars? Why didn't they adopt the laws of Monesh?"

"Ah yes, our mortal enemies, the Zochars...they rejected the laws of Monesh, they rejected his laws because they involved the self-sacrifice of perpetual migration. No, they rejected his laws, choosing rather to live settled lives in caves. But lacking in any skills to start true lives again from the ashes of our lost ways, they became the lazy kinds of men to whom evil appeals. They refused to reject the malice which entered our world with the appearance of Melzar. And so they make their vile livings by preying on us, their one time brothers and sisters."

"And they...sacrifice some of their victims?"

"You know of this?"

"Yes, from a picture we saw in a cave."

"Yes, they offer these unfortunate captives to their vile god, Melzar. For some reason, they believe it pleases their master. Yes, his ways burrow into them, like hungry parasites into creatures."

"Do they believe anything else about these, um, these rituals?"

"No, nothing else, nothing else known to me. But that is enough for us to know."

"Oh, Olkar," Aashi remarked, "I feel so badly for your people. I feel your pain."

"Yes, you would," Olkar replied with a slight smile, "you of so tender a heart."

Appearing embarrassed, Aashi lowered her head, just for a moment.

"Olkar," she said looking up, "I have a delicate question as well. May I ask it?"

"Yes, please ask me your question."

"Well, once I saw, or thought so at the time, a tiny man, a tiny man who vanished into a crevice."

Olkar smiled on hearing this.

"Ah, you think of the Absim, a legendary people...how strange that you would imagine seeing one...our children sometimes say they see them. Yet we adults see only tiny swirls of dust bearing wind that one sees sometimes in drier parts."

"Is there a legend attached to the Absim?"

"Yes, a small legend as befits a small folk. The legend has it that the Absim were once as tall as us. But then, after our catastrophe they began to shrink! Why they began to shrink the legend does not say. Ah, but the Absim, not knowing the reason they shrank, became afraid, so afraid that they quickly slip away should other people appear. Some, the legend says, became so thin and light that the wind at times whisks them away. But now, my friends, can you tell me about yourselves? Where do you come from?"

"Ah yes, Olkar, my new friend, let's just say we come from a faraway world to visit places like yours, to learn of other peoples, and in return share something of ourselves."

"Another world, truly?"

"Truly."

"Then, you have certain powers…"

"Small powers, Olkar, small powers. At the end of the day, we merely represent people like you, people filled with curious questions of life."

"Questions of life, yes, of life…some of life is solid and real, some less visible, some condensed into legends, as the legend of the Absim I just shared with you."

"Mm, an interesting legend too, Olkar," Aashi grasped her cue. "But now, if you don't mind, my husband and I are tired and so feel the need for sleep."

"Ah, so you feel sleepy right as the sun drops below the horizon."

"Yes, Olkar, yes we do."

"Be at peace in your dreams, Aashi," Olkar said, two flattened hands joining in front of his face.

"Be at peace in your dreams, too, Olkar," Aashi replied, modeling his gesture.

And so, filled to the brim with new and vibrant impressions, Dan and Aashi were shown to their tent for the night. Inside, feeling an ancient assurance from colored tent walls, both let out a sigh of relief but also of bemusement.

"Phew! What a load of conflicting info we gleaned in one short encounter!" Dan began. "Just where do you want to start here, Aashi?"

"Perhaps at the beginning, Dan? A disaster befalling this planet?"

"Yes, a disaster of cosmic proportions…"

"The real beginning for the people we now encounter."

"Yeah, the real beginning for a people whose ultimate origin lost in the mists of time. So, concerning this new beginning, the cosmic disaster itself, though odds of such an event minuscule, sounded plausible, at least, in and of itself, that is to say."

"Well, yes, I'm inclined to agree with you, Dan…the part about Melzar perhaps representing an emotional and psychological reaction to overwhelming disaster...a disaster on a scale we can scarcely imagine."

"Yeaaah, something like that. I mean, when faced by crushing disaster, people first grope for a reason it occurred. Then with maddened frenzy, they just might seek to blame someone for all their troubles...and so this Melzar guy pops up...likely a projection of sorts, a projection of fear and death given tangible form...and such a cosmic disaster likely sparked a keen awareness of evil. The kind of cosmic event Olkar talked about...how does one explain forces of nature which disrupt not only matter but cosmic reason itself? It would certainly make sense in a human way to see a massive disaster like that as an act of sheerest malice...and malice as such not part of nature...hence again the evil being persona takes on form."

"Yes, an evil being, although nature itself is not always benign."

"Meaning?"

"Meaning the obvious, Dan. For example, a male grizzly bear will kill its own young if encountered. Darwin may say it does this to weed out potential rivals while it can, to perpetuate its sense of being the species. But then again, Darwin would also say that animals protect their young to help perpetuate the species."

"Huh, okay, natural evil. But hey, that still sounds all wrong...the destructive edge of nature can't really be given a malign will, can it? City flattening storms, things of that nature, they just happen. True, a type of perfection exists, holding things together, but still, our universe, so very much material, and us but sticky clumps of ancient star dust. No wonder our lives can get messy, messy too the way things often work."

"Well, whatever the case here, Dan, these overwhelmed people zeroed in on the negative edge of nature and gave it some kind of human voice. So then that

Melzar fills the bill. Ah, but what of our Monesh? Does he sound real to you?"

"Yeaaah, I think it safe to say Monesh an historical figure...with the added aura of a man who saved a people from further disaster."

"Right. But now, the hard part, Dan. How, how did these people come to believe that day and night continue on like they did in their long lost past?"

"A pointed question, Aashi. How indeed do they think they're in that kind of normal world? Mind over matter?"

"Mind over matter you say? Oh, Dan, that's more an expression than a working construct, and used in such a casual way...although it does make me think of a few noted researchers, pioneers of thought, they were..."

"Pioneers of thought...yeah, nice choice of words, my love, those chocolate dipped words of yours..."

"And chocolate the one thing the agency forgot to pack! Oh, but almost as good as chocolate, some words which James Jeans, the British physicist and mathematician used to describe how things work: the universe begins to look more like a great thought than a great machine."

"Ah yeah, great thought, that. And some lessor known theorists toyed with the notion of mind stuff, mind stuff mixing with matter...or in other words, mind as a principle diffused throughout the universe. Still, ideas like that on an individual level don't suggest a stage type act where a magician makes things appear and disappear through the power of thought alone, meaning that Olkar and his people can't change the planetary reality here just by thinking. But there's something in the mind/matter relationship that we should keep in mind."

"Alright, Dan, we should keep it in mind, at least. Yet for now, such a concept is way too theoretical for us to use...ah, wait a minute! Something more concrete here.

What about us? What about our falling into a dream pit where subconscious and conscious minds freely mixed?"

"Yeah, okay, so you now suggest the Dreshi have somehow incorporated a planetary anomaly, the center-point dream thing, into how they perceive reality?"

"Yes, but before you voice the obvious objection that dreams are dreams and cannot affect how we see the world as a whole..."

"...or cause actual changes? Stop a minute, Aashi, and think about what you're saying. These people, they appear to go through a day/night cycle, conduct their lives along such lines...but, and here's the big but, when they enter the night side of this world, do their dreaming minds actually illuminate the path they tread with the light of day?"

"Mm, well, perhaps they stumble along, the reality of darkness having its effect, with them *believing* they walk in the light of day, but in an awkward way they blame on fatigue or some such thing."

"Ah, possibly like hypnosis? Their leaders suggesting beliefs when they're in a trance-like state, planting a post-hypnotic suggestion?"

"Um, well, now that you spell it out in those terms, it sounds somewhat unlikely..."

"Aha, wait! Here's an alternate thought. Maybe some kind of planetary memory persists, leaving ghostly traces of its past activities for the Dreshi to somehow tune into?"

"Actually, Dan, I'm not going to blow away that dust bunny of a thought, because right now, even fluff has a kind of substance compared to nothing."

"Oh? And why the sudden kind streak?"

"Because your new idea made me think of something more concrete and plausible, at least to a point. Think, Dan. By being in more or less perpetual transit around this planet, the Dreshi's movement itself could somehow induce a rotational feeling, the dream element greasing the wheels of this process, so to speak."

"But how, Aashi, how would it all work together?"

"That, Dan, is the question of the day, and the day here a perpetual one."

"Yeah, a long one, indeed. What a mess! A smorgasbord of thoughts, when all we really need is the soup of the day. And consider this: we haven't even begun to address the thorny issue of the Zochars, a people whom Olkar says worship Melzar. Do they perceive a day/night cycle of some kind? They sleep in caves, that at least would induce the feeling of night. But then again, they might be fully aware of the endless day above them…ah, they must be aware of the true state of affairs here, Aashi, or they wouldn't set up their ambush points and altars so near the twilight band!"

"Ah, yes, a good point, Dan…but of course, not conclusive proof."

"No, not conclusive…for that kind of proof, I'd need to sit down and talk to one of those Zochars."

"Over dinner, which might be you?"

"A big naw naw, Aashi, no pun intended. Because, my love, a human sacrifice needs to be whole and unblemished."

"That lets you off the hook, Dan, you with residual pimples…"

"Ya know, something tells me the Zochars have no sense of humor. Dang, what a handicap to have, and one that makes contacting them all the more risky."

"You must be kidding, Dan. Really, you don't seriously propose an attempted communication with those people, do you?"

"Could answer lots of questions, like why they sacrifice humans and why their altars abut the twilight band of this planet."

"Wait a minute…what about that pictogram?"

"What about it?"

"Well, if the sphere represents this planet, then the cone on top could represent the cone of night...this making sense if you rotate the pictogram 90 degrees right and then down, picturing the sun off to the left, like on the horizontal solar system chart I mentioned before."

"Ah yeah, so the cave position would have the sphere above the sun."

"So let's just say the sphere represents this planet, with the cone arising from it...starting at the sphere's midpoint from that angle, meaning its dusk and dawn bands, if in fact it represents the cone of night, the shadow of night cast by a planet receiving sunlight on its opposite side."

"And these dusk/dawn bands where the Zochars set up their altars...ah, and so maybe they hope their sacrificial victims ascend that cone of night up to its peak, there to somehow bring back a normal day/night cycle? Huh, pure conjecture, Aashi, but it has at least the ring of the plausible. But I don't see how it helps us."

"Yes, hard to see how it helps us, Dan, but conceivably it may be of use to us later, if our guesses are on the mark."

"Yeah, *if* our guesses on the mark, a mighty big if."

Two days after these events, Dreshi rites complete, the party resumed its long journey. By the end of the first day, firmly now in the twilight band, life began to change. For one thing, the wind, which before had been just gusty, began to slightly curl in a curious way. At first this effect scarcely seen, towards the end of the march cloud bands curled freely. The temperature began to dip as well, in the not unpleasant way of an autumn evening. Then too, when certain cloud swirls tightened, showers resulted. Rare but seen as well, lightning bolts lit up the sky when cloud swirls meshed with swirls of dust blown in from the planet's day side. Finally, stars began to fill the sky, twinkling in harmony an ancient coded message.

In the next few days, the sense of mystery deepened. Almost wholly dark now and cooler, the swirling clouds became more intense. And next a surprise – birdlike creatures appeared. Some swooped down on the party, curious, or so it appeared. Then, when some of the children tossed up scraps, the deftest birds would snatch them.

Plant life thrived on the night side as well due to an odd adaptation: plant leaves had an ultra-thin metallic coating, this derived from minerals in the soil. Then these leaves caught starlight for photosynthesis. Not only that, some plants had leaves aimed at a larger focal leaf they sent reflected light to.

Onward into night they plunged, stars blazing in darkness. And, in this galactic zone, they burned brighter than stars from Earth. Constellations emerged, the natural result of human brain wiring…and maybe bird brain wiring, too? For Dan suspected now that might explain this bizarre bird migration from sunlight to darkness, constellation maps within the brains of even daytime species. Unsure of the reason for this, flight itself might explain it – that being aloft in the air, land passing below, bird faculties fine-tuned to what above. Possibly then, these birdlike creatures had an inborn need for stellar orientation. So, just maybe the birds of this planet needed to know where they were in a big way.

At any rate, as their trek continued, at about the time they drew closer to the planet's opposite hemispheric dream center-point, an odd thing happened. For like some invisible wind, all felt an opposing force to their forward progress. Day by day it increased, until at a certain point, Olkar altered the party's course thirty-five degrees northward. This lowered the resistance, although it still felt on their right sides. When Dan asked Olkar about this effect, he said he could not speak of it. But he did tell Dan that after several days, they would return to their original course along the equator. So, minds puzzled into pretzel shapes,

Dan and Aashi huddled together after dinner to probe these events.

"Well now Aashi, whatta ya think of this second honeymoon I've arranged for ya?"

"Oh, it's a dream come true, Dan! One superlative after another. The truth is, though, I'm still working on our first puzzle, the way the clouds here swirl the way they do…and interact with these sharp stars in such a novel way…oh, wait, perhaps not so novel, Dan. No, not so novel…because, my love, they remind me of Van Gogh's painting, *Starry Night,* but ours a living version, ever changing."

"Huh, yeah…that evocative painting."

"Yes, evocative. But no painter created these patterns. So what principles might explain so engaging a night sky?"

"Yeah, what principles, indeed…hmm, well now, Aashi, might have to do with the stark boundary here between day and night."

"Meaning?"

"Meaning that cooler airs draw in warmer airs, resulting in convection, you know, like in a fluid, the warmer fluid rises, the cooler fluid sinks, resulting in circular motion. And remember, air is a fluid too, just a super thin one."

"Mm, okay, and with an endless supply of warmer air, a high pressure system, and the cooler air a low pressure system, the flow would generally be from sunny side to dark."

"Sounds about right. And of course it rains more here, vegetation lusher, though far from a verdant rainforest, by a mile, in fact."

"Still, it's comfy enough for birds. Who would have thought, birds on the flip side. I always picture birds in sun, only creepy owls at night. Oh, but then again, with those spangled stars above, our birds have the light of thousands of suns to swish by under."

"Yeah, the soaring of birds, wind under their wings and...hey, wait! That's it, Aashi! Or possibly a part of it, at least."

"A part of what?"

"A part of that repelling force we felt as we drew closer to the night side hemispheric center-point."

"Meaning?"

"Meaning that like a magnet, the sunny side positive pole of this planet attracts objects around it. Conversely, the negative pole repels, pushes upward and outward. So what we have here is an ad hoc pair of poles behaving like a magnet. Funny, when the normal north/south poles ceased their spinning, the axis they represented then defunct, somehow this oddball pair of poles came into being."

"A possibly helpful idea, Dan...perhaps a little amazing...this by default pole system of yours...our dream thing, I'm beginning to see, a secondary result of something more physical and planetary."

"Yes, the dream thing might factor in here."

"But now, this proposed pole system of yours...so an ad hoc axis of sorts runs from bright to dark side pole, um, in some sense wanting to spin? Replacing the defunct true axis? Meaning that a planet which once had spin in some sense *needs* its occurrence?"

"Yeah, but are you attributing will to a planet now?"

"Only in the sense of stored geological energies, you know, like along a fault line on Earth, the tension created demanding release in the form of earthquakes."

"Stored geological tensions needing an outlet...okay, and on this planet, somehow artificially frozen in space, those tensions still exist and seek an outlet...a spin of some sort most of all..."

"But now, not only does the original, natural axis push for spin, but the new space freeze created axis, too."

"...resulting in slight but steady tremors being released from that stored geological tension, but in a criss-crossing way as old and new axis both seek to transmit spin, like two radio transmission towers operating nearby at the same time."

"These two conflicting transmissions having effects on the minds of the people here, and in some inexplicable way producing the dream pole effect?"

"Dang! That was a fast two step dance process, my love. Maybe a gram or two of truth to what we just said."

"Possibly so, Dan. And so a physical, planetary effect transcribes itself into a force which acts on sensitive minds in more subjective ways. But now, pertaining to our *geographic* situation, suppose that the opposite center-point of this planet, according to the new pole and axis scheme, if we had reached it, might have induced *bad* dreams?"

"Not entirely sure on that one, Aashi...all this stuff so tentative, as yet, that is."

"A point well taken, Dan...still, something to keep in mind, don't you think?"

"Oh yeah, something to keep in mind for sure."

***

Resuming their long journey through the night side of the Planet Alcenta, Dan and Aashi had adapted well to the long night effect. Yet Aashi still stood mesmerized at the sight of the swirling cloud night sky, a common sight here. That and her fondness for birds made her journey rewarding. Dan, on the other hand, still mulled over the angles so far considered. Aashi's speculations intriguing him, he tried to see if they meshed with other angles. Yet in the end it proved an exercise in frustration, no big picture emerging. Still, a gnawing sense grew that something about this rare planet hinted at a method to its madness. Yes, somehow, he thought, all these info bits would mesh in time to form the big picture. In the meantime, they both had to wonder at the lack of major friction as they passed through the night side. But they had shunned the major enigma here, the dark pole itself. Olkar's silence giving them pause, Dan concluded that zone where the action occurred, but not the kind of action nomads favored. Yet maybe that pole would enter the picture here yet.

However that may be, at length that special day arrived. Entering into predawn light, an amazing thing happened. Bird flights became more frequent, as if some powerful force now tugged on their passions. And so they flew towards that band of dim light, it inducing evocative bird songs. But reaching a certain point, skittishly they swerved back into starlight. Then desire flared up again, making them swerve dawn-ward. But then the tug of stars above dried new songs in their throats as darkness won out.

Stirred and saddened by the sight, Aashi felt their pain, that sun-ward longing thwarted. Aware now too of a sense of deprivation, when she and Dan together walked into predawn, the warming swirls of wind, bearing scents of the world of the day, quickened their pulses. On the day the sun peeped over the horizon they held hands and wept, convulsed with first time feelings. Snapping out of this mood, they scanned a pristine horizon. To the east, growing light showed rocky plateau country. A glance back to the west now made them shudder. Next looking southeast, they feasted longing eyes on a daylit range of mountains. Then, right at this point, Olkar called for a three day pause to perform certain rites.

Next the two became aware that Olkar, while experiencing day and night like the rest of his people, likely had a sense of what really occurred. Dan wondered how this mental process worked. For the Dreshi had found their way through the dark as if seeing clearly. And, while bright starlight in fact shed discernible light, their bearing and behavior demonstrated a real effect of the sun. Dan decided he could not rest until he understood this baffling process.

But then the unexpected happened. As Dan and Aashi withdrew from their party while they conducted rites, six knife wielding men seized and tied them. Swiftly they were taken into a cave. Down they wound into blackness, Zochar eyes dark adapted. As for the terrified pair, void defined their new world, that and their captors' foul breath.

Soon they entered a chamber lit red with torches. Thrust onto the cave floor, there they sat not knowing what to expect. But Dan noticed a curious thing. His trembling hands stilled as he peered about, curiosity of what would happen next eclipsing his fear. Good thing too, as any chance of survival called for clear thinking.

"You!" an entering man snarled. "Where are you from? Where are you from and what are you doing here?"

"We come from a place very far from your land. We came in peace to learn the secrets of nature. We also seek to befriend the new peoples we meet," Dan calmly replied.

"You are not welcome in our land! Oh, but wait, we will, in a short time, welcome your contribution to our greatest of efforts."

"Um, our contribution to your greatest effort?"

"Yes, our greatest effort, our effort to understand things we cannot see. Yes, things we cannot see but can with our inner eyes. Oh yes, in the last stretch of time, not long, we have sensed a new force from above."

"A new force from above, you say…to what end do you seek to understand this new force? What effect do you think understanding this force would have on you?"

"We are unsure, but we hope this understanding will free us from the need to live in caves. Something in our world is wrong…our knowledge of Melzar tells us so. Yes, Melzar, our great god…long ages ago he arrived here. Melzar brought knowledge of the stars and beyond to our small lives. He gave us laws and rites."

"Ah, so you…you sacrifice people on altars?"

"In the past we did this. Melzar taught us a life has meaning only if serves the truest knowledge, his true knowledge. So to be most alive, to pierce the skin of murk which keeps our lives small, we must serve Melzar's needs before our own. This we do in rites which give us power, the power to pierce the mists of time and awaken our true lives."

"Ah yes, power. So, you did this in the past, this sacrifice thing, but now you do not?"

"No, we do not. Something new entered our feelings, not long ago. We now make use of captive lives in a much better way."

"Uh oh…a much better way, you say?"

"Yes, a much better way. Now we dig long tunnels running east to west. In these tunnels, we lay bound volunteers in a line, feet touching the head to their north and so on, in male/female lengths of 20 people."

Dan shuddered at the thought of what came next. Aashi shut her eyes and would have blocked her ears if she could have.

"So what happens next?"

"At the head of these long lines, four people's heads join the top head to form a semi-circle. So then the life force and mental power of all these people find a powerful focal point, a focal point aimed straight up at the heavens."

"To what end, might I ask?"

"We are uncertain of the end you speak of. But something we cannot see but feel nudges us to do this. So we keep these bound victims alive as long as possible. But bound people, lying motionless on a cave floor, do not live a long time. So we always need more people. So, it is still a type of sacrifice, after all."

"Right, more people…aha, but us two – we are *not* people. We come from a far away world. Just look at us! How different we appear, you must agree. So we, as nonpeople, will be of no use to your um, your spiritual project."

Their captor paused in thought. He could not deny their appearance was not like his own: less than five feet tall, thin bodied and thin headed, with a long nose and small mouth.

"You, both of you," he then pronounced, "you will be held prisoner while our council discusses this matter."

Having pronounced his verdict, they hustled Dan and Aashi to a nearby chamber with a thick wooden door. Door swung shut, next they heard a plank thud into place, locking the door. Stunned silence reigned a moment before Dan spoke up.

"Look, Aashi, I know things don't look good, but at least I bought us a little time to think of an escape plan. So please, gentle heart, don't panic. We still have a sliver of time to act in."

Aashi, absorbing Dan's words, calmed down a bit.

"Yes, you're correct, Dan, at least we have a breathing space here. But these people, so cruel. How do such things come about? How do people turn into hurting machines?"

"A question for the ages, my love, a question for the ages. Soon we can discuss it at length, but as for now, we don't have long to discover a means of escape."

Here Aashi looked again at four stone walls, feeling the pain of her tight bonds.

"But is that even possible, Dan? Bound and locked in this dark chamber? Um, perhaps it's time for us to locate back to our base?" she ended with a note of fear in her voice.

"Ah yeah, abort our mission, miss out on the dawn band effect...yet in balance, weighing our situation with care, I'd say the danger now outweighs whatever we might learn...okay, Aashi, let's go for it."

And so the pair went through the mental prep and next launched themselves. When they opened their eyes, their cell walls still contained them.

"What happened, Dan? Our sequence didn't work. We're still in danger! What went wrong, do you think?"

"The dream pole effect...somehow it interferes with our withdrawal. Entering this planet was no problem, like arrows we pierced right through its effect. But now, embedded in this planet's quirky system, leaving is like trying to pull an arrowhead out. One simply cannot do it without assistance."

"But who will help us, Dan?"

"Stay calm, Aashi. A means of escape exists, almost always an overlooked angle a captive can exploit. The *real* question is, can the captive discover it in time?"

But just at that moment, a small semi-transparent man walked into the room. Appearance-wise, from what they could see of him, he looked much like a Zochar but of course much smaller. Then too, his transparency suggested a man disappearing in slow degrees.

"Ah!" Aashi exclaimed, eyeing the slip of a man, "the Absim, your people's name is the Absim! Dan!" she added, turning his way, "An Absim! My eyes played no tricks on me back by that pool."

"Yet by me a neat trick played, wouldn't you say?" the small man said with a smile. "Oh, but my two friends outside – work they do on unlocking the door."

Moments later the door with a creak opened up.

"Now, freed captives, move with haste you must! Out of this darkness I lead you now, my light held aloft."

And so, in a pleasant state of disarray, Dan and Aashi, unbound, followed the strange little man. Issuing back into predawn light, with haste they approached the Dreshi camp, stopping on a bluff overlooking the scene.

"How? Why?" Aashi began. "How did you know we were prisoners of the Zochars? Why did you free us? You so secretive a people."

"Yes, from probing eyes my people hide, and so my vanishing act when you first saw me."

"You? The same one…amazing! But why did you and your friends track us? Oh, and why, why do you hide so well from the Dreshi that they think you a legend?"

"Hide we must from other types because, well, we have not the right words to explain our existence to them. And prompted we were by the danger you faced to track you. But our most important reason was…this wounded world of ours you are not from?"

"No, we are not from your world. Is that so obvious from our appearance alone?"

"Yes, obvious from appearance alone. And before my people's disaster, understand we did how life could exist on far away planets."

"But why the tracking and rescue?"

"You being from another world, hope we did you knew the way to help our wounded planet."

"Oh my, I am so sorry to disappoint you, um, and what might your name be?"

"Instan my name, Artor and Libnid my friends."

Here all three of them bowed.

"So pleased to meet you all." She smiled back. "My name is Aashi, and this is my husband, Dan. Oh, but as I was saying, I'm so sorry to disappoint you, but while we truly do come from another world, we lack the needed power to help your planet."

"Oh, so disappointing, but happy still I am to have helped you escape. Know the Zochars we do from long observation…and in our long lost past, one and the same people we were, along with the Dreshi."

"Wait a minute, let me see here," Dan cut in. "The Zochars – they're a bit over five feet tall, only a tall Zochar approaching that height. The Dreshi, well, the Dreshi appear taller than the Zochars, but not by much. And you, the Absim, clearly the smallest of all. Mightily I wonder now of a possible reason for this size division."

"Ah, Dan, how observant of you. Yes, a reason exists for this difference. Wandering nomads the Dreshi are, as you now know. And due to their unending journey and other cosmic forces, perceive they do day and night where none exists. They come the closest, of our three kinds, to being what all our people once truly were."

"Amazing. What else here?"

"By spending half their time in caves, the Zochars also sense day and night. So, some physical stature they have retained...though living underground has dulled their minds...that and the absence of a starry night sky. For apart from the faint music-like rhythms stars produce, alone the sight of stars affects our minds well...and this the Zochars lack, venturing not to the night side. Oh, but see my people do the stars, as into that pure night at times we venture. Ah, and sadly for them, Melzar's force, like a poisonous flower, in their hidden depths blossomed."

"Huh, tainted flowers, alright. But now, Instan, what about Melzar? We suppose that due to the trauma your people experienced in the past, he symbolizes the forces of evil in nature, if we might express it in those terms. Or in other words, he has no real existence himself, rather existing as a principle in the minds of believers."

"Confirm or deny I cannot, your observation, Dan. Full knowledge we lack to make a certain judgment on the nature of Melzar."

"Oh, but Instan, your people cause me the most curiosity of all. For not only did you shrink, but you at times appear almost transparent, although now a little more substantial. Can you explain this?"

"Um, partly I may, Dan. Forsake the lands of our birth we could not, for one thing, to endless travel. Also, while slip we do into crevices, under the sun we must live, a sun to us much loved. Oh, but now a source of pain it is to our kind, we the people most altered by our planet's past disaster. For as you know, a world which moves not at all lacks dimension and depth.

"This being true, lack dimension we did in time and so began to shrink, over generations. And, with our shrunken size, began we did to experience our internal dimensions as lacking, almost as if a tall building of metal girders slowly began to collapse, in the process losing geometric structure. Oh, and discover we did that lacking internal symmetry, a being cannot exist."

"But we have a contradiction here, Instan. For if a being can't live without the internal symmetry you speak of, and you losing yours…"

"…then why do we exist? Well, Dan, exist our missing symmetry does, but in another world, or another dimension. To plainly state, by a universal law, the dissolving of a being's inner dimensions in one world means its lost symmetry must reemerge elsewhere."

"But why?"

"The symmetry mathematical, exist it does apart from one single life. So when we dissolve completely, into a new world we will emerge, the nature of which we now may only imagine."

"Aw man, Roger Penrose said something that your words just brought to mind, not the same in meaning but possibly related in a sense…"

"Roger Penrose?"

"A great physicist on my home planet. He believed in a timeless idea regarding mathematics as stated by Plato, another great thinker on our planet. Plato believed that mathematical laws exist independently, apart from an individual human mind, in some transcendent place, or ah, maybe no place at all? That last bit a notion of my own."

"Ah yes, Dan, see I do how these two ideas, um…"

"Share common ground?"

"Yes, share common ground. Oh, what a marvel our universe is!"

"A marvel indeed, Instan. Too bad our minds so finite in nature...and yet, hints of the big picture seep through, matters all connecting in mysterious ways...so the Absim, Instan, I now see, of all your planet's peoples, are the wisest, cosmically speaking."

"How unwise we feel, Dan, but for the compliment thank you."

"So, here we sit, snatched from an adder's den, out in the partial light of day, speaking of large matters...while not long ago we faced a short, grim future...how can we ever repay you, Instan?"

"Stay alive, you must, Dan, if you wish to repay us. For if learn you do of a way to heal our wounded planet..."

"You'll be the first to know, Instan. Oh, but those other captives...what a terrible fate to fall into Zochar hands. Might there be a way to set those hapless captives free, do you think?"

"Give we will your inquiry our thought, Dan."

"In the meantime, Instan, might I prevail upon you to join us as we rejoin our host, Olkar? Mighty pleased he would be, to make your acquaintance. Ah, and not only that, but just maybe the time is right for a summit between your two peoples, you know, to firstly get acquainted and secondly share ideas for improving the lot of your long separated peoples."

"Oh, but how ingrained our habits are, habits which tell us to hide, we think for good reason."

"High time to form a new habit, my friend."

"And habits can bind us or free us, depending," Aashi added.

"So better to form new habits that point at new freedoms," Dan concluded, smiling.

"Oh, and speaking of freedom," Aashi snatched back her theme, "I get the feeling, Instan, that recent events have potential, latent power which your people may use to their advantage. But you have to *choose* to grasp these events, make full use of them, let them take you where they will, trusting that new place a better one than this."

"Obscure this concept is to me. Ah, but understand I do about making choices, one's day full of them."

"Yes, Instan, simple choices and large ones as well. And large events have happened here now, events with hidden potential for good. Think of it this way: a beautiful river flows by, a river which flows into a desirable land. Now, you can build a boat and ride the current to that desirable land – or not, depending on the decision you make, your freedom of choice."

"And that river you might be?"

"Well, perhaps, but the events emerging now – they could be the real river."

"A pleasing image, Aashi. Convince me you have to attend this special meeting."

And so this unforeseen meeting soon came to fruition. Instan alone attended, the better to ease Dreshi shock at seeing a legend alive. Yet after the initial shock wore off, the two leaders warmed to each other. And, when Olkar learned that the Absim as a whole were fading away, sadness filled his heart. When he asked if any efforts could prevent this kind of displacement, Instan wanted to say that only the return of their planet's rotation could reverse it. And yet he held back, knowing how the Dreshi had overcome this rotational lack in their non-physical way. Instead he told Olkar of a new and better world awaiting his people. But then, when Dan brought up the matter of the Zochar prisoners, pained expressions followed.

"Yes," Instan noted, "sad the fate of those prisoners, so beyond the reach of our help. Determined fighters the Zochars too, and masters of deception. Their tunnels fortified, a face to face attack they would repel. Little I know of the answer to so painful an issue, Dan. Known to Olkar too our limited field of action. Even so, as I said before, think my people will of a possible plan."

"Yes, sadly I must agree my new friend. We Dreshi fight on the surface to prevent these abductions, and there have much success. Yet the Zochars move about with stealth, blending in with shadows in some uncanny way. Oh, but to enter their caves and challenge them underground...I cannot yet conceive of an action plan that would be effective...only if we knew of all entrances and exits to the caves they use, but this would take much time and exploration."

"Too bad, Olkar, too bad," Dan replied. "Just to save those people alone would be the primary goal of any such action...but ah, something else lurks in the underbrush here that I can't quite put my finger on, having to do with a new type of ritual involving the Zochar prisoners...but as that issue can't be properly addressed now, maybe we should adjourn our little meeting. Truly, I suspect, each people here has learned much from this unexpected contact, and needs time to digest these new impressions."

And so the meeting ended. Yet after a time of refreshment, Dan, feeling troubled, arranged a private session with Instan.

"Yes, Dan," Aashi began, "what you said about the prisoners...that bizarre ritual and its possible meaning...and as you said, some hidden thing prowls about in the shadows. I feel it as well."

"Feel it as well?" Instan inquired.

"Yes, Instan, my instincts tell me something is amiss, pertaining to this issue. Recalling now what that Zochar spoke of, that they knew not what they did in an, um, in a conscious way, but rather felt an invisible longing."

"Tell me more, Aashi."

"I wish I could, Instan...but only feel a trace of meaning here...oh, but wait. Your people, before this disaster your people had charts of your solar system, correct?"

"Yes, we did."

"Well, imagine now a chart which puts sun and planets on a horizontal plane, sun on the left, planet Alcenta on the right."

"Done."

"Now, imagine your planet's oh so slow counter-clockwise orbit inching forward so slowly that only passing generations get any sense of shifting stars."

"Yes, locked our stars appear in their positions."

"Ah, and the beauty of space, no up or down there...so now, shift the solar system chart to the vertical position, sun at the bottom, planet Alcenta at the top. Next imagine your planet as the tip of a line from your sun."

"Visualizing this, what comes next?"

"Next come our prisoners, in rows of twenty, running west to east, feet to head to feet and so on. So then, with the vertical chart shift, in relation to that imaginary straight line, we now have columns of men and women standing up, semi-circle star burst of five people atop. When we do this, and us being at your planet's equator, these people stand at the tip and forefront of that straight line, at the center of that small rounded tip, for all practical purposes frozen in position, visually representing, at least, a freeze in time."

"Visually representing a freeze in time...a symbol of time so poised, like a sculpture which depicts a hand throwing a ball."

"Yes, Instan, a symbol of time so poised. Oh, and in tandem with this oh so slight forward movement through space, we have a static wake on the planet's night side. Mmm, taken altogether, that paradoxically static wake, and one remaining the same width as your planet, is like a spear shaft, your planet the sphere tip, although this spear tip round...all of this in a sense practically frozen in position and symbolically, at least, frozen in time."

"Most amazing the image you paint."

"Oh, but Instan, most crucial for us here and now are those captives. With no awareness of their symbolic arrangement, they feel only pain. Ah, but the Zochars symbolically and with no pain, place themselves in this frozen in time pose, for reasons they can't quite grasp with their conscious minds."

"Amazing, Aashi!" Dan broke in, "yes, you do indeed paint an amazing picture for us. And I see how that picture blends with what you said before about that imaginary sun rotational spirals, and all...at least I *think* I see how it blends...your whole dang premise all based on an unknown force which your imagination wants to express...still, you know, you tread on shaky ground, my love...still kind of dream stuff..."

"Well perhaps a quick review will help solidify things a bit, Dan. Think of those columns of captives, where they are, on the planetary dawn band, dividing equally east and west hemispheres, and furthermore at that band's precise center, yet on the equator as well, putting them on the precise north and south hemisphere division point, making their position a double center! So, my imaginary solar rotational spiral, coming from a sun rotating clockwise, in some sense interacts with this planet's super slow counter-clockwise orbit, this inducing the symbolic almost frozen in time spear thrust forward, on the point of striking its target but never really doing so...ah, and these solar spiral waves would also interface with those columns of captives, on the center of the round tip of my spear."

"Okay, maybe that helps a bit, visually, at least. But remember the dream pole effect, and how it still distorts our thinking. We all want to help those prisoners, but still, your captivating theory could be wrong."

"Oh, but Dan, this planet is all wrong! For starters, it being frozen in space this way an impossibility, according to the known laws of physics. No other planet like this may exist in our galaxy, perhaps the whole universe! In this sense my scenario, in some obscure way, could well fit – your Zen paradox thing back again."

"Zen paradox and captives on the round tip of a spear thrusting forward oh so slightly …too much to envision at once, Aashi."

"I agree, Dan. But later it could make sense."

"Yeah, maybe. In the meantime, for the next few days we should poke about this campsite, looking for clues to help us solve this mystery."

***

And so, an unusual event occurred at this time. With the meeting of peoples estranged for so long, a festive air arose under that static dawn sky. For with the approval of Instan, a number of Absim appeared, open to sharing their lives with the Dreshi. The Dreshi, in turn, braced by this infusion of novel ideas, opened up as never before. Now, at first Olkar had resisted this meeting of peoples, fearing new ideas could weaken his people's longstanding survival traditions. But then, refreshed by his meeting with Instan, he gave his approval to the mood of the times. For the winds of change had blown in and could only with effort be thwarted. Maybe a whole new world would arise from this meshing of cultures, an amalgam of hope.

Dan and Aashi joined in, drinking in the upbeat mood of lonely peoples meeting. Yet soon they felt it time to leave, this an Alcenta affair. So together they probed the lands about camp, for a possible new angle on freeing the prisoners. At this point too, Dan noted how this horizon hugging sun produced deep yet luminous shadows. Soon he noted as well how the dawn light changed the effect landscapes had on him. Dawn on Earth so brief, minds there had little chance to fully tune in to its light band. But now, from this frozen low angled light, a new perspective emerged.

So Dan began to take note of the high mountain west, slightly south. Almost it marked the hemispheric center-point, right on the band that divided day from night into equal half spheres, west and east. Then too, the mountain being on the equator, it arose near the spot which further divided the planet into north and south hemispheres.

The main peak, striking enough, high and snow-capped, the lessor peak ascending halfway up its northern slope next caught his eyes. Soon Dan began to imagine a snug high valley between them. Next he divided both mountains into geometric designs, this division in turn reflecting mathematical structure. Doing some calculations in his head, their result confirmed his hunch. But Aashi, noting Dan's mood, pulled the plug from his think tank.

"Snap out of it, Dan! You've been staring at those two mountains for over an hour now, a symptom of self-hypnosis."

"Huh? What? Self-hypnosis, you say? Aw come on, Aashi, gimme a break, will ya? And me right on the verge of some kind of insight or other. Then you jar me away with your petty concerns."

"Oh right, Dan. Your health and well-being a petty concern? Whatever you say, my love, whatever you say."

Dan remained silent a moment, knowing what would come next.

"Alright, Dan, go ahead and regale me with your brilliant insight."

"Hasn't quite fully formed, Aashi, but ah, it has to do with a bowl shaped little valley nestled between those two mountains there."

"A bowl shaped little valley? How can you see *any* kind of depression between those two mountains from this angle?"

"Now don't get mad when I say this, but I'm gonna sound something like you by saying that I imagined it there…and confirmed it mathematically, based on sheer geometry alone."

"Let's go with your second idea, Dan, it sounds more substantial."

"Okay, say we have a bowl shaped little valley or just a depression in the gap between those mountains…a half sphere, if you will. Consider this in light of what you said to Instan a few days ago, actually the matter we discussed before, the solar system viewed vertically thing, sun at bottom, planet at top. Anyway, add to that the lines of prisoners running horizontally underground, west to east, feet pointed west, heads pointed east, in effect making them stand up in relation to their position on that chart, as you fit it into your scheme, and consider how close in location they are, this proposed little valley and those prisoners."

"Mmm, so what comes next?"

"Add to that what you noted then, these same human vertical lines facing incoming imaginary rotational waves from the clockwise rotating sun at the same time this planet's counter-clockwise orbit moves onward so slowly that in effect we have a near perpetually frozen spear tip in space ever close to striking its target but never really doing so. Add to this your observation that the point of your rounded spear tip, meaning this planet, where these hapless captives stand, is on *both* the equator dividing northern hemisphere from southern, and the dawn band dividing day from night on this stationary planet, all so perfectly centered, and presto!"

"Presto what?"

"Aw now Aashi, why'd you go and spoil it for me?"

"You don't know what, do you?"

"I know only that such a strategic indentation, such a hidden dell a suspect point, all other factors considered. This being so, let's hike up to that cleft between the mountains and check it out."

"A bowl shaped dell? You want us to climb that steep rocky slope just to see if a bowl shaped dell exists between those two peaks. Have I left something out, Dan?"

"Only yourself, if you'd rather not go with me. Olkar and his people plan to linger here for several more days, so that would work out."

"You know I'm going with you."

"Okay. Just checking."

And so, with a mix of trepidation and high excitement, they set out for their goal. Reaching the slope and beginning their climb, with the weaker gravity here they made good time. At first noting the pleasing new richness in the more plentifully rained on vegetation, they shifted mental gears as they neared Dan's destination. Imagine Aashi's surprise when not only did they discover a half sphere shaped depression, but smack in its center a metallic half sphere, looking like an observatory dome but with no telescope slot.

"My God, Dan, how did you…"

"Like I said, Aashi, I imagined it first then confirmed it with a quick dose of math. But that metallic dome…a stunning surprise for me, too."

"Yes, a total surprise. However that may be, Dan, your insight bore fruit. But now the real question: just what is it we have discovered here? Whatever it may be, appearance-wise, it bears no relationship to anything else on this planet…um, with the one exception of this bowl shaped little dell."

"Yeaaah, sure looks unique for this planet. So shall we, my love? Shall we walk up and knock on the door if it has one?"

"No other option here, Dan, we both such curious types that to just climb back down this mountain equals the unthinkable."

"Ah, but your thought assumes the unbreakable, meaning you think us immune from harm should something hostile dwell in that thing."

"Lead the way, Dan, or should I say Iron Man?"

"Shoulda, woulda, coulda, but too late for that now, Aashi. Let's get goin'."

And so they did, winding down a smooth slope right up to the anomalous structure. Approaching the site, they saw a mid-sized dome, about fifty feet high and the same in width. The metal, with the appearance of a silver-titanium mix, looked so perfectly shiny and smooth that without a second thought Aashi strode up and touched it. Reveling in the sensation of pure smoothness, she next gave it a rap, feedback telling her the metal thick and solid. Then too, its perfect smoothness produced a perfect finish which Aashi found more pleasing than that first sip of wine. At this point Dan joined her, feeling compunction too late for not thwarting Aashi's approach to potential danger. But now he too stroked the dome, feedback telling him that if fingertips had taste buds, this surface would taste like strawberry shortcake with whipped cream on top. But then he drew his hand back, advising Aashi do likewise.

Next they walked around the sphere, looking for some kind of door. Yet all appeared seamless and smooth, as if this structure an enormous half pearl. A few more circuits around producing nothing new, they sat before the dome and mightily wondered.

"Well, Dan, any brilliant ideas now? This is your imaginary dome, after all."

"Aw now, Aashi, let's not start with that imaginary bit again. This silver pearl looks real enough to me...although now that you broach the subject again, might it possibly be some kind of projection from afar, one so perfect that it comes complete with sensations for eyes and fingers?"

"You hint at an unbelievably advanced technology, Dan, but your notion provokes me."

"Provokes in a good way, I hope."

"Yes, a good way, Dan. Aha, and now it strikes me this is no metallic half pearl but a whole one, the half we cannot see underground…almost as if it had landed with impact with this exposed half the result?"

"Don't know how to answer that one, but your idea has impact on me. But yeah, seems to make sense – one perfect orb before us…ah, but now, what if this sphere no manufactured item at all but an *actual* cosmic pearl?"

"A product of nature somehow? Nature on a cosmic scale? Ah yesss, your idea has strong appeal, Dan. And yet, even if true, I still get the sense of mind somehow relating to what we now see, and I mean the mind of a lessor being, no cosmic one. Somehow, yes, I sense a connection here…

"Ah, but now, if I were a painter, Dan, how wonderful to paint just one perfect picture like the object before our eyes. Yes," she continued, standing up now, "only here, right here, I would have painted the hint of a perfectly round seam suggesting a portal inward."

So Aashi did just that, tracing a large circle which began overhead. Then, with a slight hissing sound a real seam appeared. Falling back a few feet it next disappeared, revealing a portal. Aghast at this development, fear and wonder competed in each for control. Yet with balance on this brink persisting for seconds, wonder triumphed. So, taking a deep breath and each other's hand, into the pearl they both strode.

Once inside the portal closed, again with a hiss sound. Knowing now the only way out lay ahead, inward they plunged. Then an amazing thing happened. For far from appearing the fairly small sphere viewed from the outside, the interior was spacious, or so they imagined, at least. In a corridor now, passageways branched off as way farther than fifty feet they proceeded inward. Yet when they turned around to see how far they'd come, the corridor vanished, branching passageways along with it. Gulping with trepidation, they looked each other in the eyes. With simultaneous sighs, onward they plunged, seeing on their left a rising staircase. Deciding it time for a climb, they ascended a series of staircases, like in a tall building yet not, as cases behind seemed to vanish. At last they entered a chamber, a polished round half sphere with a dark slate floor. On its walls were images, some disappearing others opening up, like expanding bubbles. Puzzled, Dan watched on. Then, wondering mightily where this whole sphere came from, an image of a fissure bubbling up blossomed. Thinking of Aashi now, the bubble shrank back down as he physically turned to face his cherished companion.

"Any ideas at all about what gives here, Aashi?"

But before Aashi could answer, a man stepped out of a mirror on the rounded wall. Halting close to the couple, he gave them the up/down size up, appearing none too thrilled by his uninvited guests. Standing still and silent, this humanoid, arrayed in a blue silken robe with curling gold design, appeared slightly less than five feet tall, on the chubby side, with a type of Mohawk hairstyle crowning his pudgy round face. Clearly he expected the couple to give an account of their trespass. As seconds passed and silence reigned, he lost his patience.

"You, you creatures have some nerve, I must say. Don't tell me, let me guess – where *you* come from, a dismal little world, no doubt, if *I* had done the same, if I had entered your home unannounced and through some covert method, I'm guessing my reception would have included some kind of crude weapon, with you all afire to use it and ask questions later."

"In times past, maybe…"

119 • Worlds Beyond the Cloud

"A *short* time past, is my surmise. And your red meat cud chewing habit still shows in your eyes, let me tell you."

"Aw man, I haven't had a steak in decades, if you must know. But now, becoming much more aware of what's going on here, I see you have a point. So, we're sorry about the trespass. We really had no idea of what this sphere all about...um, but now that the subject popped up, just what is this sphere, exactly?"

"What do you want it to be?"

"That's it? That's your answer?"

"Yes."

"Okay, let me retrench here. Ah, maybe you could tell me who made this sphere?"

"Not me."

"That's it? That's your answer?"

"Yes."

"But...you know where it came from, don't you?"

"Ah, a glint of intelligence here. How refreshing. So yes, I do know where it came from, and yet I do not."

"There you go, Dan, your beloved Zen paradox."

"Zen paradox?"

"Yes, a type of thinking which transcends cultures, despite the Japanese title we often use to describe it. It deals with contradictions, um, for example in the phrase, *bright shining darkness.*"

"Oh, how cute...but I do see some method to your thinking after all."

"But why? Why do you live here alone in this well-hidden sphere?"

"You mean, why do I live in this *hidden until now sphere?*"

"Anger duly noted. And again we apologize. But now, you know about what goes on down below. I know you do."

"Then why did you ask me if you already knew?"

"To get the double confirmation I just got. So my next question is why do you, as some kind of superior being, appear unconcerned about the cruelties going on right under your nose? You do know of them, you must, being so clearly superior."

"And being so clearly superior, you must realize my ultimate goal is understanding and knowledge. And now, don't tell me, let me guess. On *your* home planet, yuk! Oh, but on your home planet, certain people study nature. So, as they study nature, do they not witness acts of cruelty, animal killing animal, sometimes with excruciating slowness? Why then do not these wise men, these scientists, rush forward to save the victims?"

"Aw look man, there's no need for that haughty tone. I don't care if your IQ is 300, beings owe each other a certain level of mutual consideration. As for studying nature, how can you possible equate animal cruelty with higher being cruelty?"

"Cruelty is cruelty, is it not?"

"Okay, alright, it is. But snap out of this theoretical framework. Right below this mountain, as we speak, people are being tortured. Don't you feel anything for them?"

"Well, yes, it is somewhat sad to consider. Oh, but the higher good here, the goal of probing interstellar anthropological mysteries, so noble an end, justifies our non-interference rule while on a field study."

A moment of silence ensued.

"A *field* study, you say? A field study? So, you, you're like an advanced version of a grad student in Tanzania studying some kind of human behaviors and rituals, only you don't give a damn if some of those people die right under your nose."

"Only because our reward of knowledge is so much vaster that the crude type of study you mentioned."

"But how did you find this planetary anomaly?" Aashi piped in. "It seems to me almost inconceivable that you somehow detected it from your home planet. Of course, you may have come across it during a random expedition. Still, something doesn't quite mesh here, um, and what might your name be?"

"Name? What's in a name? What is it about a name that requires one to dispense it on demand?"

"Oh, well, let me see…common courtesy, perhaps?"

"Huh. Orton, my name is Orton."

"Well, Orton, let me be perfectly honest with you. Something here doesn't quite mesh with your story so far. For one thing, this orb we inhabit at the moment…strikes me as so far advanced in construction and function that as a base for an anthropological study…I mean, to put it in terms my husband Dan might use, it's a little like using an atomic bomb to kill a fly."

"Well put, Aashi," Dan smiled.

"In other words, Orton, I suspect you hold something back."

"Ha! So *that's* how your kind operates, is it? Break into someone's home and then accuse your victim of being dishonest! How does that thought 'mesh' with *you*, Aashi?"

"Well yes, what we did was wrong and we apologized for it. But here is the real issue between us now, Orton: hundreds of prisoners face needless death, while you, with the power to prevent it, do nothing, all in the name of a higher good, knowledge. Yes, we are all capable of deception, under certain circumstances. But this life and death issue has rendered null and void less essential grievances. So again I must emphatically say that your words don't quite ring *wholly* true, at least. Please, please do not let custom, habit, or inclination prevent you from clearing the air for us here, just a bit."

"Just a bit, eh? Just like that you expect me to trust two complete strangers."

"Who else *can* you trust, Orton? You have no communication with the subjects of your study, that much is apparent. In fact, you and this sphere seem a unit of sorts. I doubt if you ever step out of it. Add to this no others of your kind appear to live here. So, logic tells us you have no one else to trust! There! Now please, feel free to tell us more."

Orton, still angry and very much into himself, could not help but be tickled by the ring in Aashi's voice.

"Aashi, you say your name is? Aashi…well, Aashi, you have, it appears, pierced my presentation to the layer below it. So yes, there is a little more to my personal saga on this forlorn planet. Now, it is true that I study from my perch what transpires below me. I also live in this sphere exclusively. That much is true. But as to my people's original mission on this planet, well, this place was chosen because of its size, disposition in relation to its sun, type of orbit and other factors which made it an ideal subject for a major study. My people, you see, had advanced to a breathtaking level. For you see, Aashi, in truth we had the capacity to, um, to intervene with this once normal planet in such a way as to produce the odd arrangement you have experienced for yourself."

"No, no way!" Dan interrupted. "No civilization could come up with the sheer forces combined with the deftness of their use to produce this oddball effect."

"True enough, Dan, no *ordinary* civilization, ours an extraordinary civilization."

"Making you extraordinary, too, I take it?"

"You take it correctly. And so you see, we, having the capacity to produce this effect, were driven by our curious natures to carry it out in order to observe and study the results."

"All this an experiment…so you could study how a lesser civilization than yours would evolve after such a fiasco…this strikes me as coldblooded, Orton, as in reptilian skulker of the underbrush."

"Oh really now, Dan, your quaint use of insult is so quite amusing. I see my estimation of your civilization must go down two more notches."

"And *I* can see that you must really like your nachos…nachos being a food so tasty one often eats too much…get it, Orton?"

"Oh, Dan, you are so extremely fortunate that I am not like one of the fictional aliens I now detect lurking in your subconscious mind, one of a vicious nature."

"A mind reader too, eh? Any more tricks up your sleeve?"

"Now, Dan, simmer down," Aashi broke in. "Speaking of nachos, this is not a macho thing, which you appear to be turning it into. Please, Dan, evolve a little. Take a break to think about that. As for you, Orton, I hate to say this, but…you, my self-deceived new friend, fit the bill, let me clearly state, of an, um, an evil alien?"

Hearing this, Orton's already minimal sense of humor hit the floor.

"Evil? Evil, you say…let me begin my response by stating that having almost never used that word myself it still has its full meaning for me, rather than the intended insult your usage suggests to me here. So now you hit me on the head with that word…just because some lessor beings die, not by *my* hand but by their own hands, while I follow the simple rule of non-interference."

"Forgive me, Orton, but I had to use that word as an, um, as a wake up call, as our people say. This means I only want you to see what goes on in your mind in a more objective way than an individual is capable of…especially one as isolated as you. Yes, self-absorption is a trap we must all beware of. Because, if we are taken in its snare, we may distort what we see in ourselves and in other beings as well. So please, Orton, take my admonition as the medicine I meant it to be."

A wall of silence descended, Orton appearing pensive. But then his eyes lit up a bit as he turned to face Aashi again.

"Ah! That's better, light in your eyes," Aashi observed. "So, to carefully proceed here, so far now we understand that your people, using massive expertise, made this planet stop in its tracks, more or less, in all respects, it once an orbiting, rotating planet. But now, again you must be honest, Orton. Yes, I can see that the study of this unusual planetary disposition on higher beings' perceptions would interest you. But again, it yet appears to me a vastly disproportionate use of highly developed power, merely to study effects on other beings. Might there be anything else, any little thing, you'd like to share with us at this point?"

Again a pause as Orton loudly exhaled.

"Well, there was a certain cosmological component of our experiment..."

"Really? And just what was the nature of that component?"

"The cosmological component of our experiment involved the setting up of an ah, an edge of time."

"An edge of time?"

"Yes, Aashi, an edge of time – partly a title of convenience, even while time and its edge were involved."

"Wait a minute, Orton, an edge of time...might that describe some sort of effect caused by the oh so slow counter-clockwise orbit of this planet which renders it effectively stationary in space, its sun's clockwise rotation in some mysterious way having a wave effect on this planet? Wait. In fact, this planet, when viewed on a chart horizontally – resembles the tip of an imaginary line in space, a spear shaft, if you will...this shaft a paradoxically stationary and non-widening wake cast as these spiral waves are blocked by the opposite side of this planet. Oh, and on the precise center of that round spear tip, the Zochars have placed their sacrificial victims in columns of people standing up vertically in relation to this incoming rotational wave effect. But our picture is so incomplete. Could you make it more complete, Orton?"

"This sphere makes it more complete...partially more complete."

"How so?"

"Simply stated, this orb was the first fruit of our cosmic experiment. You see, Aashi, once we succeeded in essentially stopping this planet and neutralizing its rotation, a strange current passed between sun and planet...but what I just said a surmise only, as we had no instruments to detect this unforeseen result...but we did see a thin long bolt of lightning pass from sun to planet...which resulted in the instant appearance of this orb."

"What? You mean your people did not produce it?"

"Oh heavens, no...it being light years beyond anything we could produce, mega-light years, in truth. So yes, and I am still uncertain, let me frankly tell you, of just how it appeared, spontaneously on this spot or something which descended from a nearby hole in the fabric of space-time that the lightning stroke opened up for a split second."

"Oh, so amazing to imagine...a temporary hole in space-time, leading perhaps to some other universe or another dimension, or no universe or dimension at all..."

"Nothing at all," Dan interjected. "Your thought makes me think of what lifelong prober of physics, Dennis Overbye, once noted. Certain physicists that he knew said nothing could be the ultimate symmetry, a gridlock of perfection, the *possibility* of everything..."

"Yes, we thought of that cosmological possibility, too," Orton sighed. "But the phenomenon lasted but a split second. We had no way of being certain what had occurred. Possibly no hole in the fabric of space-time had opened, the sphere appearing spontaneously where it now rests, for all we knew. Oh, but in either case, whether from a hole in the fabric of space-time or spontaneous formation on this planet, the sphere's effect was immediate and profound, producing a most astonishing warp in space-time near this planet persisting to this day."

"An amazing development. Please do continue."

"Yes, amazing. After the primary effect and resulting planetary convolutions, the new order of nature began to stop quaking, settling down so much that one man alone was deemed sufficient to conduct the study, that one person being me."

"So you've been alone," Aashi cut in.

"For ages now, literally."

"No contact from your planet whatsoever?"

"No, not for the longest time. You see, Aashi, you have now squeezed out of me the following confession. My ultra-advanced people, a model for this galaxy to follow, or so we once believed, destroyed themselves in an all-consuming war. So sad, and we for so long believing we had evolved beyond so base a state."

"Oh, how terribly sad. And you, the sole survivor of your kind?"

"As far as I know. Oh, there could have been other survivors, but none ever showed up here."

"So self-absorption on your part would be inevitable, given the givens of your unfortunate situation."

"Yes, given the givens, Aashi," Orton smiled.

"Oh, but Orton! If you have been alone for ages...I mean, you don't look thousands of years old to me. How can this be?"

"Again I have no answer to that, Aashi, other than my connection with this enigmatic sphere. Ah, yes, and in its fresh state it appeared white hot, slowly cooling to rounded perfection. When I later learned of the entry trick and came inside, everything was blank, empty...something like the nothing you just mentioned, Dan, nothing, nothing in the sense of no thing, no created thing...yet a fountain of something? The issuing of something from nothing? Or the possibility of such an issuing? Oh, well, whatever the case, it soon responded to me, taking on a certain interior form. Oh, and vastness I have experienced in this sphere, let me tell you, vastness beyond comprehension, yet intimacy, too. And so it became part of me, or I part of it. Other than that, I cannot explain my vast lifespan, although it's a lonely life…but then again, not quite. In this sphere I feel a sense of connection, fulfillment, even, and so never leave it."

"Now look here, Orton," Dan responded with heat, "you appear to be painting a picture of yourself airbrushed of blemishes. For one thing, you describe your relationship with this sphere in glowing terms, only hinting at the vast power potential angle here. So let's be honest. If, in fact, you ever managed to totally merge with this thing, would that not give unimaginable powers to a single finite being? For another thing, your passive acceptance of the Zochar's recent mass human sacrifice still rubs me the wrong way. It leaves me wondering firstly why this mass scale sacrificing just recently started and secondly how you interpret its meaning. You study such goings on, don't you? And I'm gonna stick my neck out here and suggest it has some kind of meaning for you. What do you say to *that,* eh, Orton?"

"Ah yes, that ancient reaction of beings of your lowly kind…jealousy."

"Jealousy? What the…look, my friend, if you think you're gonna throw dust in our eyes by raising up a false issue, forget it. The power thing I mentioned – it makes you nervous, doesn't it? Doesn't it!"

"Anger doesn't do it for me, Dan…something I advise you to keep in mind. Just think for a minute, if possible. What if you're right about what you just said? That I have immense untapped power at my fingertips? If that were the case, Dan, a softer, more respectful tone on your part would be much more appropriate than bluster shot my way from your position of abysmal weakness compared to me even just now, with only partial sphere powers at my fingertips."

"Aha! Candor at last. Thank you, Orton. And so, now I respectfully request that you highlight this man/sphere relationship you just spoke of. With far greater possible power maybe in the offing for you, what would your personal goals be? No, wait, let me take a crack at that question first.

"Okay then, Orton, honest confession. If I had lived alone for centuries, my own people all lost in a massive war, and power at my fingertips, possibly growing by the day, well, under those circumstances, I might be tempted to grab all the power I could and eat it raw for breakfast. Why not? What would I have to lose but my loneliness? I mean, with that kind of near total power, I could project my image from planet to planet, awing less developed folk with cosmic wonders, awing them so much that cults would arise to worship my name, not even including my own magnificent presence. Yeah, just one projection would do it. Then my devotees would thrive on my brainwaves alone, brainwaves so magnified that they travel through space and time. Wow, just to imagine, millions calling on my name, in tones of fear and love, offering their all to curry my favor – a major antidote to loneliness, wouldn't you say?"

"Let me reiterate, Dan, and please do pay attention this time around. If your position were mine, I would at this point be realizing that in the presence of a man who can take what he wants at will, I would somehow plug up that black hole of a mouth of yours. Where does such a black hole lead, do you think? Do you really want to find out, mm? It can be arranged, Dan, it can be arranged."

Here Dan stopped in his tracks as the message sank in. But then his irrepressible spirit rebounded as a new thought occurred.

"You, you, Orton – you're Melzar! that so called Melzar, aren't you? You, *you're* the one who started a planetary cult ages ago, and now the Zochars thrive on your brainwaves alone, no need for you to leave the safety and comfort of your sphere. Wait, something else lurks here in the underbrush, doesn't it? Something, something rare enters into the equation here. Would you care to share that new equation, Orton or ah, Melzar?"

"Something rare indeed, my tiny molded clay friend. You see, Dan, that warp in space-time near this planet – just recently it has shown signs of renewed activity. And, as it showed these signs, my Zochar followers began to alter their sacrificial ritual into the one we see now, suggesting to me that aided both by planetary factors related to the dream pole effect and my own enhanced brainwaves, they have intuited a coming event of some kind. So, Dan, I was forced to ask myself, why this change in ritual? Why now this suggestion of actual meaning to these sacrificial rites? Well, think, could it be the hole in the fabric of space-time theory for this sphere's appearance is correct? As the small warp in nearby space-time suggests? And if this fresh activity should provoke a reopening of space-time fabric, then more power could be released into this sphere. Only a theory at this point, but one best not ignored."

"Huh, you sure know how to overlade a plate with a single spiel...oh, but wait, isn't there a caveat that goes with your power grab, Orton?"

"What do you mean, a caveat? *I* am in the position of power here, not you."

"Okay, Orton, it's like this: the Absim, a people you appear to have deliberately tuned out as despised weaklings, the Absim know something you don't know. So how does that feel, O All Mighty one?"

"What do they know that I don't know?"

"They know that a byproduct of staying in one place on this planet is firstly a physical shrinking of their beings, and then an internal structural collapse in an abstract, geometric sense, and so their growing transparency. Oh, but secondly now, they take heart at the knowledge that by a cosmic law they have discovered, this bleeding away of internal structure drips into a parallel universe, specifically another world where their internal structure reassembles, meaning their internal structure as a whole remains mathematically intact and undying."

"Ha! Those tiny things can hardly think at all. What does a termite on your planet know? And even if their supposition is true, well, good riddance to them, I say."

"Sure about that, Orton? You look to be somewhat under five feet tall now. Were you that short those ages ago, mm?"

"Oh, well, but one naturally shrinks a little as one grows older."

"But I thought you said you weren't growing older, aided by this super sphere from beyond."

"I, well, I have not aged that I know of…all thanks to this sphere."

"Ah yeah, and what about this sphere? Could be a chunk of eternity itself, one you've lightly toyed with all this time, while raising yourself up as an evil god demanding human sacrifice."

"Heed my warning, fool! My patience wears thin."

"Oh, so you're getting thinner, too? Expect the unexpected, is an idiom on my planet. So then, if and when that hole in space-time opens up again, maybe your internal structure would be swallowed right up into it, to emerge into a world where I'm pretty damn sure you wouldn't have squat when it comes to cosmic powers, or even everyday powers. Oh, but maybe a peanut sized you would be left behind, not exactly the type of fearsome being that would maintain its Zochar following."

Dan's forceful choice of words had an effect on Orton. For just a moment, fear flashed in his eyes, eyes which then fell onto a small metallic sphere mounted on a base, like a small work of art. Seeing this, Dan quickly surmised it might have a function Orton needed. Thinking then of how the sphere itself had responded to their presence as they entered, he realized that Orton had far from perfect control of its whole potential. Lastly realizing now that he and Aashi faced danger, thinking fast he grabbed the small sphere and Aashi's hand.

"Aashi, quick! Back the way we came."

Off they then dashed, the corridor opening before them. When they saw the seam reappear, they knew they had almost escaped. But hot on their heels ran Orton, furious now, and much desiring the missing piece of equipment. But then, as all three entered the light of day, several things happened at once. First the globe in Dan's hand disappeared, followed almost instantly by the sphere. With the sound of a hiss and a rising cloud of vapor, it simply vanished. Orton, stricken on witnessing this, fell to his knees. But then he too began to disappear, first wilting and then smoking, ending up as smoldering ash on the ground. Each, it appeared, orb and occupant, could not exist apart from the other. So then, without a second thought, Dan and Aashi bolted for the mountain slope and freedom.

Reaching the broad lands below, they sped full tilt to Olkar's camp, feeling now its presence a safe haven. Many people milled about, looking up at the mountain. Some claimed to have heard an explosion, but all now saw a rising plume of ash. Olkar, seeing his friends, rushed up to greet them. Dan then calmly briefed his friend on all that had transpired on the mountain. Aghast by what he learned, Olkar invited them into his tent for herbal tea refreshment. Soon replenished and calmer, all then sat outside, gazing again at the mountain perpetually under dawn's light.

Next they talked of life and hope, even on this ever static planet. They mused as well on the lessons taught by would be gods gone awry, and what it meant to be human. For human in a broad sense includes all thinking beings in the stretches of space. Aashi, in accord with her nature, pointed out how longstanding isolation had unbalanced Orton's mind, and how he'd still shown glimmers of kindness. Still, his cruel abuse of the Zochars in the end defined the man. One could only imagine what he would have become with super human power.

And, as it turned out, the Zochars were the high point of this event. For with Melzar's transmitted presence gone they came right out of their caves like children seeking guidance. And so the Zochar's prisoners soon regained their freedom, grateful to be alive in a world with people like Olkar and Instan.

The Raindrop Sea

As Dan and Aashi remained locked into the planet Alcenta's unique dynamic, the other half of their bi-locating selves, on Proxima Centauri b, had simply vanished. This unexpected complication of course set off alarm bells. How their crew had brainstormed for an explanation. Yet after several sessions, they still came up with zip. Now, bi-location, by definition, presupposed a baffling simultaneous split in personal existence. But Bretori had explained to them that often in actual practice, more of the person might enter into a more engaging second location. But a total immersion of person there rarely occurred. Even so, Bretori lastly suggested they work on this issue themselves for the time being. So then, at the end of their last brainstorming session, only Captain Grieg and Doctor Solander lingered in the meeting room. A wall of silence descending, both strove for clues.

"Damn it, Brent, just doesn't seem possible, two substantial people going up in a puff of smoke," Captain Grieg sighed.

The captain, untypically hunched over the table, appeared less tall that his six foot two stature. Then too, athletic looking face drawn tight, hardly now he oozed his usual bravado.

"Cheer up, Max. Things'll work out, I ah, I sense it in my femur," the doctor replied with a smile to lift his friend's spirits. Brent, shorter and older than Captain Grieg, still looked present enough for a man in his 50s. "Ah, and here's a thought. Could be they haven't outright disappeared from our compound here. Could be something of them lingers here yet, to reappear at the right moment."

"Yeah sure, could be something like that...but Brent, does that not suggest fresh cause for concern? I mean, if they've stumbled into some kind of mess on the planet *I* sent them to explore? Off kilter place like that bound to be unstable and risky."

"Now see here, Max, you can't go blaming yourself for sending them to that particular planet. Made good sense in a scientific way. And hey, those two – how they work so tightly together, like print on paper. Two for the price of one, a rare combo of a team. If anyone can worm their way out of a jam, it's Dan and Aashi."

"Sounds about right, Brent, yeah, it does." The captain smiled at last. "Dan can be mouthy but he still has some spine…but it didn't help to hear Bretori say we're on our own on this one…him tied up in another all-consuming venture of his own. Maybe in time he can help us."

"Yes, could be in time…aha, but here's a fresh thought, my friend. Just possibly, Max, Bretori knows those two have a handle on the situation?"

"Ah yeah, a fresh thought…a real turnip sprout of a fresh thought, if true. Oh God, what I wouldn't give for some boiled turnips with butter on top."

"Yeah, sure, sounds um, sounds almost good to me, Max, a culinary work of art. Maybe we can genetically modify our carrots?"

"Sure sure, you're the doctor, know all about gene splicing, things like that. Damn, but back to our immediate concern, what you just said could be right. In fact, knowing Bretori's style now, maybe like an old prof, he wants his students to spread their wings and grow to the point of soaring flight alone…yeah, maybe the case, ah, which for some reason makes me think of that thing we saw while passing through the Oort Cloud."

"Ah yes, that shining little ice thing in space, apparently on a course in the general direction of Earth…no comet, for sure, as some supposedly form in the Oort Cloud. So baffling…a shining bit of something in the midst of interstellar space, H_2O, it registered…too bad we couldn't have gotten closer to really inspect it...our readings so faint from that distance."

"Yeah, on the faint side...all we really got telling us a perfectly shaped globe of H_2O, 25 miles in diameter, glowing faintly, proceeding at a steady rate."

"So you wonder now at that interstellar anomaly?"

"Don't you?"

"Yes, Max, now that you refresh my memory, I do still wonder about it...yeah, and it leaving a particle wake of some kind...appearing to me to spin on its tiny axis, not sure why it would do that..."

"Spinning on its axis...ha! Who could tell from that distance, Brent? No one else perceived any rotation. Come on now, Brent, fess up. You'd tippled yourself while on duty, right?"

"Not in a million light years, Max! And you know better than to suggest so egregious a breach of conduct. No, it just seemed to me so faint but true at the time...and if so, just think, what would have set it to spinning? And what about the glow it gave off?"

"No argument there, Brent. A light bouncing glow it did have...what the hell could have caused that? What kind of space body was it? No meteor or comet shaped like that or on a straight course in deep space, straight as an arrow....an icy H_2O ball, other things mixed in, maybe an ice and rock projectile?"

"Alright, Captain Grieg, here's the deal: we two, we go on a bi-location jaunt to that glop of H_2O in space...any liquid water in it? No, that would take heat...but let's take a jaunt there, find out for real just what it is. And look, it's not greatly far from our planet here, a fair easy target. So let's deck ourselves out in the right kind of gear, and inspect that mystery blob up close and personal. And you know what, Max? I'm thinking now that just about any new thing that we learn out there would somehow be useful."

"Damn! Now why didn't I think of that? Yeah, oh yeah, it's high time we both got our feet wet with this new kind of space travel...and what a mystery to plumb...possibly that object in deep space holds more useful information stored within it than an entire planet. Deep space nature can work that way, you know."

And so it began for this fresh team, first assembling the micro-compressed gear they would need for their venture. And tiny and far off as that ice globe was, a world of sorts it would be, with gravity enough to walk on. If they grasped its hows and whys, what secrets they could uncover. Even so, they set a seven Earth day time limit on their mission. If no useful information had been gleaned by then, back to their base on Proxima Centauri b they would return, there to hang tight.

Next landing on their target, spacesuits on, the first thing they did was set up their settlement bubble on a slick icy surface. Quickly accomplished, they entered the antechamber, and next the main chamber. With ice to feed on, their miniaturized O_2 unit swung into gear. Soon they desuited, relaxed, and got their bearings, looking out first at purest space, then down at the ice sheet.

"Now *that* is what you call a risky shift!" the captain quipped. "From the relative comfort and safety of our base to this, ah, what the hell *is* this thing, Brent?"

"Hard to say, Captain...ha! But the damn thing rotates slowly, as I said."

"Good thing I thought better of making a bet. What else we got here?"

"Well, we got solid H_2O ice, Max, no other kinds of ice mixed in, and um, uh oh, take a good long gander below."

"What the hell? Liquid water, below this thick sheet of clear ice."

"You got it, Max. What a gall damn anomaly we just landed on! Ah, and judging from initial readings, this

25 mile wide…thing is a nigh perfectly shaped sphere of ice, with a sea, I suppose you could call it, under this thick sheet of ice."

"A sea, eh? Got salt in it, does it?"

"Just a trace, Max, not enough to make real salt water. Guess it's a fresh water sea, or just a round lake?"

"Huh. Some sea. Just think of salt and whales going together, like salt on fried eggs. Well, but they're only semi-type whales."

"Yeah, living in a semi-type sea in deep space. Anyhow, something at this thing's core produces light and heat…ah, what's this? Our ice contains tiny crystalline structures, maybe explaining why we can see through it like glass? Like no ice I've ever seen."

"And a core to this thing, eh? Obviously an energized core…damn! Like a huge drop of pure water way out in deep space…know what it makes me think of, Brent?"

"Fire away, Captain. Whatta ya see here?"

"Reminds me of how a drop of rain on Earth forms, from scads of micro-droplets, into one large drop, speck of dust at its core."

"Ah yeah, stroke of genius, Max…a possibly helpful image for us at the get go here. I wonder, can such a process ever be duplicated in deep freezing cold space?"

"Well now, let me see…crystals of ice in space, sure enough, water ice and other kinds…so there's issue number one. Any such space drop…could it even be made of pure water, as this one appears to be?"

"The question of the day, Captain."

"Any instrument readings yet?"

"Yeah…the core is a crystal-metal mix, spherical, highly compressed for an object this small…damn, the compression alone would produce some measure of heat…and if enough to get the metal white hot, then light appears, shining through crystal…which appears to be the case, oh, and the stuff at the core, diamond! Actually tons of that stuff scattered about in our universe, including diamond planets."

"But what causes the compression at the core of this thing? Not enough gravity produced here to account for major compression."

"Nothing we know of to date, Max."

"Well hell, nothing would surprise me just now."

"Oh yeah? How about a lifeform in this thing?"

"No way! What kind of a lifeform?"

"Readings suggest a large, whale-like creature, but unlike any whales we know of on Earth…these guys not breaking the surface to breathe….they breathe through their skin like some frogs do! But outrank frogs on the development scale by oh, a factor of a hundred. Small creatures and plants exist below us, too."

"What? No lily pond a la Monet?"

"No, not yet, anyway. Oh, wait, our instrument now shows electrical discharge at the core."

"What the hell accounts for that?"

"Ha, yeah, what accounts for that…hard to say. Maybe some kind of particle bombardment reaching this thing's core?"

"Right, science made up on the spot. And our instrument – no readings yet. Damn piece of government issue crap! If Earth were still in its buzz-saw capitalist stage, you can bet we'd have way better instruments."

"Only you, Skipper, would bring up politics in deepest space. But look, we have our work cut out for us here. Lots of things to learn in so short a time. Let's get squared away then and make this mission good to go."

"Copy that."

And so the explorers set about establishing base. On the following day, they observed with care the objects and events just noticed on the first day. To begin, the ice itself, crystal clear, proved a wonder in and of itself. For the tiny shards of diamond crystal it contained gave it a definite optical effect. In fact, Doctor Solander took to peering hard into it, perceiving the depths of clear water below. But how did this self-contained little sea replenish itself to prevent stagnation? Well, the animals below would produce carbon dioxide, the plants oxygen. And currents no doubt resulted from the core's fiery presence. Then too, the core's internal electrical discharge at times broke out of its outer shell, injecting electrical energy into the water, this likely inducing at times molecular rearrangement. Those same external discharges passed through the water as a weak current, reaching this tiny world's ice outer shell. At such times the clear ice glowed whitish iridescent. It soon became clear that core and ice shell shared an intimate bond, maybe involving more than electrical current.

This current, it appeared, did not adversely affect the whales, as both men now chose to call them. In fact, Doctor Solander began to note a positive effect on the whales, or so it appeared. For during these times of electrical transfer from core to shell, they would form circles and rotate round and round, like earth kids on a merry-go-round. When the current ceased, the circle dance stopped. Could it possibly be that those creatures played an intermediate role in this electrical transfer? If so, what did it mean? What secrets could they learn to enhance their understanding of current and future ventures from their deep space base on Proxima Centauri b?

By day three of the mission it became clear that a dive into that space drop of a sea was the next logical step, spacesuit doubling for diving gear. Through a small passage in the ice shell, the diver could be lowered attached to a tether. Their hope here boiled down to this: by beeping a transponder underwater, maybe a curious whale or two would be drawn to the diver, something which happened on Earth. Then, neither had a clear idea of what to expect, other than a firmer understanding of the nature of this lifeform, in itself a major achievement.

Captain Grieg, of course, gave himself the honored role of diver. So, burning a small hole through the ice with their light beam tool, Doctor Solander fed line to the descending man. Down to 200 feet, the captain activated his transponder. An hour elapsed with no response. At that point, the captain took a sample of the water for the good doctor to analyze. But lo and behold, just then three smaller whales appeared, about 40 feet in length, emitting sounds or whale songs, not unlike on earth. Lastly, signaling the doctor it was time to retract him, up though the ice he then splashed, landing with a light thud. Suit off, panting as though exhausted, the captain took a moment of rest.

"What? What is it, Max? What happened down there?"

"Sure as hell wish I knew, Brent. Damn! Just not the right guy for this type of mission, after all."

"Now there's a first, admission like that from you. So why the change of heart? What happened down there, Max? Start with something easy. What did those things look like close up?"

"Yeah, well, easy up until that point, this mission was...so ah, yeah, whalish they looked pretty much, except for the bony plate like things on their upper heads...on the reptilian side, that look, although their skin smooth, almost silky smooth to look at. Huh, the eyes, though, no fish or reptile eyes...deep and dark with glints of light."

"Intelligent, are they?"

"Oh yeah, but in a way incomprehensible to me."

"Gonna have to explain that one, Max."

"Right, well, they made these whale-like sounds, clicks and whistles, sounds of that nature. Now, maybe they signal each other with these sounds, or communicate in a vestibular way, you know, gestures and movements."

"So how *did* they communicate?"

"Well, with me, some kind of mind to mind transfer. Really weird…flashes I saw, images of some distant things, bodies in space…"

"They communicated with you mind to mind?"

"Yes and no, yes, in that it damn sure wasn't verbal, or grunts, or anything like that…and their brainwaves…if that's what I felt, wow, almost had substance."

"Almost?"

"They did leave me with the impression of a planet and a journey…"

"Their journey?"

"Yes, Doctor Solander, their journey. You see, my friend, this whole damn thing is some kind of a spacecraft."

"No way. Tell me the truth here."

"Wish I could, Brent, but that's about the extent of our communication – picture of a journey and a planet…which planet, I wonder?"

"Well, they're aimed in the general direction of Earth, and we have oceans there. Oh no, whale refugees in space? Travelling at a rate that'll take 'em one hundred years to reach Earth, if that's where they're headed?"

"Huh, don't know what to say to that, Brent. But could we not learn more from these creatures, communicate some more…oh, but this time with you! Sure as hell not me again…yeah, you might learn more, and that includes how this damn ice coated raindrop of a spacecraft actually works."

"Sure no real spacecraft, Max."

"Yeah, but it's acting like a spacecraft, or mimicking one, and it does carry a crew of sorts."

"Right, an ice ball spacecraft, with a crew of pixilated leviathans…maybe looking for a real ocean to live in? And, while not real whales, they're close enough for rock and roll, at least in deep space. Zoologists would flip their wigs of course, but we must take a more comprehensive view of life beyond the Oort Cloud."

"Right. But yeah, some kind of thinking goes on in those brains, well above what it takes to do a few tricks at a sea-themed amusement park."

"Well, there goes my theory that all advanced thinking type beings by some cosmic law have to appear in humanoid form...although I've heard it said that every creature bears a certain resemblance to God, *the* form imprinter, according to some."

"Now hold your horses there, Doc. No time to wax philosophical or theological, or whatever, when what we really need is car wax."

"Can't wait to hear you explain *that* one."

"Well yeah, if this ice ball's their car, then if they want to really strut their stuff, they'd buff it up first – number one, in a decorative way, and number two, the metaphorical wax allowing it to smoothly do its thing with energy transfers? Must have other kinds of functions, too. What can this thing do, all told? Sure, it looks primitive...but then not, balance of multiple simultaneous sorts and energy exchanges going on here. So, if we figure *that* one out, then we understand what its crew all about."

"Sounds plausible, Max. But now you're taking about a full-blown mission for us, not just a seven day jaunt on this space decoration."

"So it would seem, Brent. And I meant what I said about *you* going down into that thing next time for further probing."

"Ahm, yes, me for further probing...not exactly part of my medical training, but hey, it could boost my understanding of astrophysics, now couldn't it?"

"Wouldn't take much to improve the ah, the grasp you have on that subject right now."

With that the two dug in for a more concentrated study. So, taking the rest of that day to hash over mental notes, next day it was the good doctor's turn for a swim. Lowered into the water, Brent opened his eyes as wide as he could, took several deep breaths, and hit his transponder. Sure enough, in several minutes three whales showed up, possibly the same ones as before. Again they squeaked and sang in their way, before one of them locked eyes with Doctor Solander. Then, a flood of information passed between the two, so much in fact that the overwhelmed doctor with a gasp had to pull back. Next, with an odd signal of its left fore fin, the whale appeared to signal its understanding. So, raised back up to their tiny base, the brave diver hit the ice floor.

"What? What did you learn, Brent? Spit it out, man!"

"What did I learn, Max? How about this: everything and nothing at all."

"Aw no, tell me it ain't so, Brent...your mind so bent out of shape you come out with a Dan line, him and his paradox shit."

"Don't know how else to express it, Max...something huge in that image exchange, something small and hard to see...maybe one and the same thing, for all I know."

"Aha. So you're saying an exchange of info took place, a two way street."

"Yeah, it did, but that creature's street a wide one, mine a narrow."

"Alright, take another deep breath and focus. I want to hear what you learned."

"Okay, Max, here's what I learned: this thing is *not* a spacecraft."

"What? Whatta ya mean, it's not a spacecraft? That the one clear impression those things left me with after my dive."

"Yeah sure, maybe like some of the other dives you've been in, right Max?" The good doctor smiled.

"Great, and now a Dan smart ass quip from you, of all crew members. Those things – they've jarred your delicate brain."

"Well, not to contradict you, Max, but the way this thing functions…has an organic feel to it, for one thing…"

"What? So you're saying it's some kind of organism?"

"I didn't say that, did I? Said it had an organic feel, is all. I also got a sense of how it functions."

"So you know how it functions?"

"Not in any purely mechanical way. And before contesting my findings, consider how an organism, in a certain sense, at least, functions like a machine."

"There you go again, claiming this thing a critter of sorts."

"I didn't say that, damn it! Keep in mind, Captain, these are fledgling impressions. Funny too, those whales thought it more important for me to learn of their home more than of themselves. Anyway, this thing, or ship, does function…crystal clear I sensed energy exchanges with purpose, as well as a type of guidance system…with mapping schemes of some kind…and ah, not radar, or probe beams, but some outward sensing organ of some kind, probing space for, ah, for something."

"For a gas station maybe? Or are you the one who's run outta gas?"

"And yet, Max, for all that, this type of mechanism/organism does not appear to know exactly where it is…or is in the process of taking bearings…"

"You gleaned all that from eye contact? While mostly I just got a headache?"

"Information yes, but in images, pictures of a sort, which told a story."

"Great. Now you sound like Aashi. What a crew to send light years from home."

"Just the right crew, Max, in my humble opinion. Oh, and one more thing: this sphere – it's slowing down."

"What? In interstellar space? For no apparent reason? Another hard sell, Brent."

"Nevertheless, that notion caught on when I dove into this thing."

"Look, Brent, you've forced my hand. *I'm* gonna have to go down there one more time in search of reliable impressions."

"Right, the ole reliable in action again. Now that should be interesting."

The Brewing Storm

As the ash plume from the mountain dell continued to ascend, the happy Alcenta survivors paused in their talk. All eyes next turned skyward as birds flew in from the night side. At first in an elegant pattern their ordered ranks broke, birds flying off alone. Some returned to the night, others circled overhead, confused. Adding to this rare sight, clouds spilled out of the night side, dropping hailstones as they swiftly flowed into light. All who witnessed this event stood up, shaken. Transfixed as they were to the sight, only in several minutes did troubling thoughts churn up. Some began to panic, others lost their bearings, as if their inner gyroscopes had been thrown out of whack. Recovering somewhat from this effect, Dan was the first one to speak.

"Okay everyone, clearly something happens here, way out normal. And now I suspect it related to the destruction of that sphere and its less than stellar guest."

"Yes, of course, Dan," Aashi agreed, "the timing here…no coincidence."

"Right. So let's not lose our heads. This might be what's behind these events: the sphere, somehow it acted to stabilize the odd dynamic of this world…meaning mainly the day/night pole effect. But what *is* the dynamic involved? How does it work? If we could answer that question, then possibly we might counteract this sudden shift in this wounded planet's forces."

"The birds, Dan, the birds…first we must learn why they did what they just did."

"Right, Aashi. Our first question here: why the bird reaction? Well, how about this for a theory…ah, wait! even more! Maybe I can explain why the birds dwell in the night hemisphere. Yeah, so imagine a time when this planet rotated and had seasons, star patterns stable but shifting with the planet's rotation and seasonal cycles. Some or maybe all bird brains contained a map of star arrangements for various reasons. Oh, but then, when this planet became stationary, the stars locked into place, unmoving. So birds on the dark side were locked into place *along with* the unmoving stars. So locked, they learned to adapt. Ah, but birds on the day side...their star maps dimmed by an always bright sun caused them disarray, even day active species, which I'm supposing on this planet, at least, had some kind of star dependence. So aimless migrations began, those making it to the dark side finding again those needed stars, birds trapped in the sun dying off."

"Yes!" Olkar agreed, standing up and pacing, "yes, Dan, with understanding like this, we can rise above our confusion! We are men, not birds. We understand certain laws, possess the gift of reason. Yes, we can fight this disturbing new force, drive it back where it came from. But how, Dan, how will we do it?"

"Yeah, how *will* we do it? Any ideas here, Aashi?"

"No, Dan, no ideas right now."

"Think back to our brief stay in that sphere...anything pop up?"

"Ah, one thing, Dan, what you said with your bluff, when you scared Orton into thinking you knew something he didn't about cosmic forces, concerning the Absim. You called the sphere a chunk of eternity."

"Well, yeah, but that just a bluff as you noted."

"Still, if the sphere truly appeared from some type of rip in space-time, then it could at least have *come from* a timeless locale."

"Well, a chunk of something it was, something clearly *resistant* of time...aha! But now, concrete and in our faces, what about our new Zochar converts? Them so confused now that they seek out Dreshi instruction?"

"So much untapped information at our fingertips! And one of their leaders right here. Olkar, can you find this man, bring him here for a round of questions?"

"A wise proposal, Aashi. I will fetch him at once."

***

Soon the Zochar leader stood before them, the very one who had spoken to Dan and Aashi as captives. Yet how his tone had changed. Almost like a child among unknown adults, he walked with slouched shoulders and spoke in short nervous clips. Seeing at once he needed reassurance in order to work with them now, Aashi spent twenty good minutes conversing with Brilech. And, with her gift for reaching out, this knotted up man in fact loosened up, enough to flash a short-lived smile to Aashi.

"So Brilech," she softly continued, "if you truly wish to help us now, we need to know more of Melzar and the sphere he lived in. What can you tell us of his nature? And what of his relationship with the sphere?"

Struggling for a moment, Brilech spoke up.

"Melzar's brain waves, they controlled us, this you already know. Little else can I tell you now of his nature. Oh, but the sphere he lived in...somehow the sphere opposed Melzar's presence."

What?" Dan cut in. "How can that be, Brilech? The same sphere which gave him long life and additional powers? You say it opposed his presence?"

"Yes, the sphere did oppose Melzar's presence by um, by acting around his will, for the good of our planet."

"It acted *around* Melzar's will? Could you give us something a bit more concrete?"

Again Brilech fell silent before speaking up.

"Maybe this will help, Dan. My thoughts, they bent around Melzar's own thoughts, as if to escape them. I sense this now to be true."

"So your thoughts *bent* around Melzar's…ah, wait a minute, Brilech, this bending, it reminds me of Olkar bending our course 35 degrees north of the night side pole. We actually felt the negative force of that pole push us away, the course change feeling natural."

"Yes! Yes! You have stirred another impression, Dan. The pole on our planet's night side – Melzar's thoughts, his brain waves, they travelled there, and other places, too. But once at that dark pole, his thoughts mixed with natural elements, congealing into an essence more lasting than a fading thought."

"What? Congealed thoughts? Melzar's thoughts *congealed* at the night pole? What might such a dubious process involve? What exactly did they congeal into?"

"Of that I am uncertain."

"Well now, Brilech, if what you say is true, then some essence of the man exists on your planet yet."

"Or a reflection of the man?" Aashi added, "a presence not alive but there in a sense? Like a reflection on water which the water somehow held onto?"

"A reflection held onto…hmm, don't know how realistic that notion is, Aashi, but it paints a nice picture in the mind.…ah yeah, wait a minute. Do you remember when we discussed simple refraction?"

"Yes, that time by the pool, you going on about a stick in the water…"

"And its bending…a stick stuck in water bending it into a slight v shape…the stick still straight, but not, as optics would have it…resulting in a split between what we *think* should be the real position and the displaced position the water actually gives it."

"Yes, Dan, a simple yet interesting phenomenon. But what does it have to do with our current discussion?"

"Yeah, what does it? Maybe something, Aashi. Just an impression in the rough here, but let me lay it out for you. But try and think of what I'm about to present here as an um, as a mental primer of sorts."

"Alright, Dan, proceed."

"Right. Okay, first, that anomalous ripple in space-time near this planet…from what we understand so far, it's the left over effect of a rip in the fabric of space-time that Orton's people unexpectedly opened up after they managed to more or less freeze this planet in its tracks. Beyond that rip? Nothing, or eternity, another word for nothing? A state where time has no meaning, in both cases."

"Sill unclear, Dan."

"I'm getting to my point here. Now, since no one actually knows how time and eternity would interact supposing some kind of infusion of eternity into time occurred, then allow me to suggest that the contact of nothing, eternity, with space-time…would produce an undefinable interface, but maybe with just one factor we could define, that one factor being refraction."

"Refraction I understand."

"Right. So first, the sphere, it comes from nothing, or nowhere, its nature completely unknown. Ah, but now, upon its contact with space-time the sphere reacts as if space-time a type of fluid, and so refraction occurs. Consequently, as the sphere descends to this planet, it has *two* positions, position one the refracted position, and position two its trajectory to this planet on a straight line course."

"But how could the sphere have had two separate courses, Dan?"

"Well, the refracted course would be the natural material course refraction would cause, conforming to the laws of physics in the material order. Ah, but the straight line course would be the result of something *beyond* the material order and its laws barreling into space-time. That sphere's sheer and wild card force would demand a straight line descent, without even the slight bending gravity might normally cause."

"Okaaay..."

"So the sphere, in an unknowable way, right after its descent, had two locations on this planet, not far apart, but distance involved, distance maybe standing in for the reality of nothing that our senses can only infer…you know what I mean, the wide open spaces vast horizon effect."

"I know what you mean."

"So this gap between the refracted location and the straight line location of the sphere…the straight line location becomes, in a sense, an alternate real location to the one caused by nature."

"Um, go on, I think."

"Anyway, like I said, the gap between these two sphere locations figuratively represents an indeterminate openness, or in its purest sense, nothing or eternity. So this nothing gap – it becomes the location of an endless exchange of spheres seeking to merge back into one, making the sphere as a whole, within that symbolic gap, nowhere and everywhere at the same time."

"Now *that's* gonna take some explaining."

"Well, for example, consider an electron spinning around an atomic nucleus. Its spins so rapidly that its location can be inferred as a probability only. So then, one could say that in a real sense the electron exists everywhere and nowhere at the same time."

"And so this gap between your two proposed spheres becomes an emblem for this possibility, being everywhere and nowhere at the same time."

"Exactimo, my love. And while both hemispheres appear as one, all this is going on."

"Um, possibly, Dan. And Orton, through his age long association with the sphere, also existed in a sense, everywhere and nowhere at the same time, if you're right. Oh, but Dan, surely you see how far-fetched your idea is.

For one thing, how did this symbolic everywhere/nowhere gap presence of both the sphere and Orton turn universal?"

"Ah yeah... how did that happen? Well, when Orton left the sphere some kind of internal knot was cut, a bond between the two centuries in the making. That bond had acted to stabilize this process, kept it within the gap confines. But by cutting that knot this contained process could no longer be contained. Ah, an analogy – a contained nuclear reaction turning into a runaway nuclear reaction."

"That analogy helps a bit, Dan. But still, we witnessed Orton's death firsthand."

"An *apparent* death? Possibly representing the shucking of his old presence, like an emerging butterfly shucks its chrysalis?"

"You ask me to believe the impossible, Dan, Orton a butterfly."

"Yeah, well, you know what I mean."

"Yes, and your idea considered together, a variation of your paradox theme. And the gist here: you appear to be saying that the sphere was not destroyed, but simply relocated...relocated to where?"

"To where, the sphere relocated to where, that's my answer. And before you object, Aashi, *where* in this sense means everywhere and nowhere at the same time."

"Again allow me to suggest that your idea may not make sense?"

"Oh, but Aashi, you're missing the point. The point here is that this sphere itself is a link of some kind, to what exists and doesn't. Just consider how it came from beyond a rip in space-time. And what would be beyond space-time? Nothing, that's what."

"Dan," Brilech cut in, "your idea – it fascinates me, makes me glow inside...but how can so wild an idea help us where we really live?"

"Well now, Brilech, if Melzar, or Orton, soaked up that sphere's attributes though his long association with it, then, he too, as we speak, might be everywhere and nowhere at the same time. If true, it can only help us to understand that he could pop up at any time in a threatening way. But with this knowledge we stand on guard. And look, yes, at first we thought he died, it certainly appeared so, but the timing, right as the sphere disappeared...I think now the sphere simply disappeared, was not destroyed."

"But if Orton truly exists in this cloud-like state, how then can he harm us?"

"Yes, true, Brilech, this process alone poses no danger to us. But if Orton learns how to bend this process to his will, it could involve risk, not only to us but to other beings, too. But this *same* risk presents us with an opportunity. You see, Brilech, if we could trick Orton into appearing in one place, supposing he learns the skills involved in so doing, we might succeed in capturing him."

"Oh, do you think capturing Melzar would also restore my planet's normal functions?"

"Ahh, no, I don't believe that issue involved here, Brilech, sorry to say. But most likely it would bring a halt to our current problem."

"But Dan," Aashi interjected, "we have a contradiction here. According to Brilech, with his firsthand knowledge of Orton, Orton may have established some sort of a presence on this planet's night side pole. If so, then that locale must be where we direct our efforts to counter this destructive event, and reestablish some degree of equilibrium to this planet."

"True, Aashi, supposing Brilech right...and he does have some firsthand knowledge of Melzar...still, you tell me, is his idea easier to believe than mine?"

"But Brilech's possibility is front and center! Your possibility is, as you yourself put it, everywhere and nowhere at the same time. You tell *me,* Dan, how could we possibly take action against so indefinite a version of Orton?"

"Yeah, how could we? Pretty nebulous stuff."

"More issues here, Dan. As you just said about tricking Orton into manifesting himself in some way – any such manifestation would be a slight one. How could we trap so slight a version of the man? And furthermore, what could we possibly use to lure him back here?"

"Yeah, how to lure him back here…and what to use as bait…aha! Here's a thought. That little orb we found and assumed lost with the destruction of the main sphere…now, it could also now exist everywhere and nowhere. On the other hand, it might possibly still be present right here on this planet in tangible form."

"Oh, but think, Dan, even if that small orb remains in one place on this planet, or appears to, what use could it have for Orton now? Supposing him alive in your new sense?"

"I have no answer to that one, Aashi. But consider our episode with him, and how his desire to get that little orb back was powerful enough to lure him out of his safe haven...like getting a turtle to leave its shell. So it must have great value to him."

"Then why wouldn't he simply return at any time to fetch it? Supposing he now has these great powers?"

"Because, my love, as Brilech himself has said, the main sphere somehow worked around Orton's malicious presence for the good of this planet. If this be the case, then the small orb, well, maybe it too acts against Orton in some way, one such way making itself hard for him to locate."

"Oh, so exhausting, this discussion! But yes, Dan, your point is well taken…and yet it would only make sense if we accept your new theory of placement/displacement? And a theory for the books it is…comic books, perhaps?"

"Aw man, ya really know how to hurt a guy, Aashi. Okay, but look, if my new notion somehow points more directly at the issue here, then by attacking Orton on *that* front, I predict the night side pole issue, the source of our current trouble, would resolve itself with our success on the main front."

"Only in *your* mind more directly, Dan! I say no way we risk this planet pursuing your half-baked scheme."

"Oh right, half-baked now, is it? Okay, the solution here: we vote, us four, majority rules. And before we vote, Brilech, consider all the angles here, how they intersect in your newly recovered and growing mind."

"Growing, yes, Dan, my mind is now growing So, forgive me, Aashi, I do well see your good solid points, but I must vote with Dan."

"Oh, yes, and so sorry too, Aashi," Instan spoke up, "but vote I must with Dan. Odd his ideas are, and yet they captivate me."

"But Instan, a painting may captivate as well, but what use…"

Aashi paused mid-sentence, absorbing her dilemma.

"Well, husband and friends, if I were to offer more objections, point out what could go wrong, it would only act to slow much needed forward action. So, let's go for it. And Dan, if you're right on this, I hereby nominate you for a Nobel Prize…or someone with more influence should."

"Thank you, Aashi. I accept your nomination. So, now the hard part: putting all this into a series of concrete actions aimed at success."

But then, as the issue seemed resolved, Alcenta's new dynamic intervened in a forceful way, thickening clouds dropping rain and hail. Out in the open as they were, and the hailstones large, Brilech, thinking quickly, offered all safe haven in his people's tunnels. Olkar leading the way for the families under his care, all felt great relief to be out of worsening weather. But then an added twist – large toad-like creatures appeared, issuing from the night side.

"Ah," Brilech spoke, exasperated now, "my first impression of our situation, it might be coming true before our eyes. Yes, it could be true…some essence of Melzar has caused this invasion, an essence driving our harmless eptons into a frenzy. How fierce they now appear, puffed up too, as if from this rare heavy rainfall."

"They resemble my planet's toads, Brilech," Dan responded, "but these no ordinary toads, more like hell toads. Great, now the creatures here are flipping out and now we have to fight them."

At that, Dan ordered Brilech to spread the alarm, have his people man all entrances and exits. Next he ordered Aashi to quickly fetch torches. Instan, now appearing confused and thinking himself little help in a fight, morosely peered out of the cave, the meadow outside at the moment free of unbalanced eptons. But then he saw that Dan had dropped his pouch of food pills, something they would all need. So thinking to make himself useful, out he dashed to fetch the valuable pouch.

"Instan! Get back in here!" Dan shouted. But as he spoke these last few words, he noticed how transparent Instan appeared. Even as he studied his friend, a gust of wind kicked up. At first Dan groaned but then he gasped and ran out of the cave himself.

"Instan! Instan!" he shouted, as Instan took off like a kite. Higher he arose, a beautiful sight in a way, yet tragic and sad. For now they'd lost a friend but even something more. For Dan had perceived in Instan's rare traits a possible way to test his far out theory. And, if his notion bore fruit, it could alter the flow of events. So in spite of the risk, Dan held his ground outside of the cave, noting Instan's course and rate of climb. But then, noting too a cluster of eptons approaching, he dashed back to safety.

Next day as the rain continued, the fight grew fiercer. But then, during a quiet interlude, Dan and Brilech talked of their hope of turning the tide of battle.

"This situation is bad," Brilech began, "but it seems to me an unlikely event that such lowly creatures will triumph over higher beings."

Dan paused a moment, admiring his friend. For just a short time ago, Brilech could scarcely speak a coherent sentence.

"A good thought, Brilech, a real good thought. Yeah, and while fighting from a cave no day at the beach, at least we can hold out for a while...aw crap, while these things overrun your planet?"

"Oh, Dan," Aashi broke in, "what do we do now? Neither of our plans may be carried out, no journey to the night pole, or whatever you had in mind to forward your plan. Ah, the old expression, events on this planet have beaten us to the punch. If we had acted sooner...but no, events simply happened too fast."

"Yeah, a situation out of control, Aashi, at least for now. And these damn bloated toads...how ravenous they appear, eating any creature in their path and even chasing us into these damn caves...several together could kill a human, the things having teeth now. And you're right, no way to make it to the night pole or activate my plan...we appear to be trapped...but then again, being under intense pressure does have certain advantages. 'Cause you see, my love, I do have the rough outline of an action plan involving Instan."

"Instan is gone, Dan. Sadly carried off in the wind."

"Yeah, but think, Aashi, feather light as he appeared just then, he could well have landed safely. And if my observation on the mark, he appeared on course to land on the mountain of our last adventure. Ah, and his transparency and anomalous nature – which fine tunes him to cosmic forces, suggested to me he's a portal of sorts, in my plan to get at Orton."

"Oh? And what exactly *is* your new plan?"

"Uh, it's falling into place, let's say. But my point is, Instan represents a window of sorts into unseen forces at work all around us. Aha! And recall, if you will, Orton's fright when I mentioned the Absim...he too must be aware, to some degree, that in truth they represent a passageway of sorts into invisible forces."

"Yes, I do recall his fright at that point."

"Right. And now, Aashi, to use another old expression, here's the bottom line: we have just one slim chance, the plan I've just hatched, at worming our way out of this dilemma. 'Cause ah, just possibly, success with my venture could put the brakes on this massive planetary instability...but no promises here, this a high risk solo mission."

"If you mean to suggest that you go alone..."

"No suggestion, my love, the way it must be, no ifs, ands, or buts. And you're smart enough to know I speak the truth. You'll be needed here by the defenders, you with your perceptive nature and expertise."

Angry at first, Aashi calmed down.

"Alright, you win this round."

"Ah yeah, that's the spirit, Aashi. We can do it."

"Right. See you on the flip side, Dan, of this upside down situation."

And so, Dan took off on his solo mission. With great relief, he made the mountain slope and began to ascend. Pleased as ever to be climbing up high, he paused midway for a quick survey. Upward he continued, thankful that the rain now intermittent, even with cloudy skies. At last approaching the dell of their Orton encounter, Dan sat down on a rock to calculate Instan's position. Some ways still above, he assumed it to be. But then, hearing pebbles rolling down from the slope, tensing up he leaped to his feet. Armed only with a light beam which could blind, rotating in a circle he looked for suspects to blast. But then, with movements heard directly behind him, Dan practically jumped out of his skin. Panicking, he spun around, frantically waving his weapon.

***

"Okay, Captain Grieg, you ready for your second dive, the dive that one ups me?"

"Rough and ready, my friend. I'm good to go."

"Whoa! You feel that, Max? A gall damn shimmy run through this watery ice ball?"

"Sure as hell did, Doc. What does it mean?"

"Greetings, bold seekers," a beaming stranger spoke as he stood in their midst.

"Who the hell 'r you? And how the flyin' frig did you get here?" Captain Grieg asked, terrified and angry at the same time.

"Tisk tisk, gentlemen, where are your manners?"

So there smiled a self-satisfied Orton, relishing the fear and confusion he'd caused.

"Huh. Where are *your* manners?" an angry flustered Doctor Solander inquired. "Where *we* come from, people knock on doors, announce their presence before barging in at dinnertime, like a few of my relations do."

"Oh, how true, how true. Excuse my rudeness. As an apology, allow me to extend an invitation to my place, right there, not far off, about 2000 of your yards from where we now stand."

"What, you mean in deep space?"

"Oh my, how quickly your kind think. But can't you see my spacecraft?"

"Can't say as I do. But calming a little, mighty curious I be to learn where you came from, there...um, and what might your name be?"

"Orton, at your service, my esteemed hosts."

"Doctor Solander here, and there my cohort Captain Grieg."

"Oh, what a thrill to meet a doctor and a captain both in one spot. Might you have time, good Doctor Solander, to examine a bunion on my right foot?"

"Sure there's anything right about ya there, buster?" Captain Grieg cut in.

"Aha, humor. I love it! What a card you are, Captain. Is that the correct expression?"

"Close enough. But now, surely you're intelligent enough to know why we're upset."

"Oh my! Did I upset you? Shame on me! Fifty lashes with a wet noodle, right, Captain? Oh, but in your planet's past, might I not have been dragged under a ship's hull encrusted with sharp barnacles, and then once again for good measure?"

At this point, having become abundantly clear that they entertained a hostile presence, Doctor Solander thought quickly.

"You know there, Orton, there are safer places for you than way out here in the Oort Cloud. And ah, let me assure you that we have little to offer you except our best wishes as you prepare to head home. Ah, yes indeed, the ole homestead, a good thought, no? What with this rounded floating iceberg thing we stand on ready to blow, oh, not sky high, way past our Earth sky now, even higher than that, I guess you could say."

"Ah, and so you possess hidden knowledge of this ice orb's inner workings, no doubt."

"No doubt I do. Oh, but see for yourself. Just peer a moment through this clear ice, at the critters below. Huh, and *whatever* you do, don't lock eyes with one of those gall damn things. Made that mistake myself, almost cost me a layer of valuable cortex."

"Valuable, ah yes, yet manure has some value on *your* home planet. And these creatures, such trifles, hardly worth looking at."

"Ha, but one of 'em's lookin' at you, don't ya know, curious crusties of the deep as they be. Oh, but don't look back! The effect way overpowering, especially for a delicate lad like unto you."

Orton, huffing, gave the doctor a sharp look before peering down through the ice.

***

"Oh Dan, please do relax. Nervous you make me with the weapon you hold, pointed at me," Instan said calmly.

Squinting and looking hard, at last Dan saw him, Instan still transparent, but less so than before.

"Instan! You're alive! I knew you would be! Tell me how you did it, friend."

Smiling now they sat down on two rocks, facing each other.

"The wind, oh, what a glorious flight! Planned it certainly wasn't, and terrifying at first…on rare occasions only does one of us get swept away like that…oh, but that wind, up the mountainside it swished me with ease, some ways higher than here. So pained and slowly I hiked down, rocks clinging to at times for fear of another long flight. But as luck would have it, or hopefully luck, in a bouldery enclave this caught my eye."

Here Instan held up the small orb Dan had snatched from the sphere.

"Well, I'll be switched! The little metallic globe from Melzar's sphere."

Hearing this, Instan dropped it like one hot potato, Dan picking it up.

"At first we'd thought this globe destroyed along with the sphere…but how did it remain here while the large sphere vanished? Any ideas, Instan? You with your semi-cosmic nature?"

"Could it be, Dan, simply put, that in the confusion caused by the large sphere's destruction, or transposition, drop the globe you did, assuming it lost or destroyed?"

"Huh, yeah, true, our perceptions not always reliable, especially in a pinch. Oh, but so high up on the mountain…how do you suppose it got there?"

"Uncertain how that happened, Dan, I am."

"Did you see anything unusual in that spot, Instan?"

"Nothing unusual, no…oh, a swirl of wind bearing dust, I saw, so high on a mountain an unusual sight?"

"Hard to say, Instan. But our globe here – its power, even though benign, we know, can be twisted around. Any ideas as to its power?"

"Difficult that question, Dan. Why do you ask?"

"To learn some clues as to Orton's powers, mainly. And you, Instan, with your semi-cosmic nature, you know of certain invisible forces, do you not?"

"My my my, I do seem to have a knack for dropping in without notice," the chubby alien beamed. "Oh, and what luck! Dan Stafford, first mate of the renowned spacecraft *Star Wing,* a vessel representing Earth's higher values."

"Well hell, Orton," a calm yet stricken Dan replied, "if I'd known you were coming I'd of tossed rose pedals on the ground you tread, as befits a man of your stature. But ah, something tells me you're not here for your coronation, not just yet, at least."

"Ah yes, sarcasm, so piercing the wit of your kind. Oh, but have a care what you say now, Dan. In truth my stature has been raised to dazzling new heights."

"You still look about five feet tall to me, Orton."

"Good for you, Dan! Pluck and fighting spirit, in spite of the odds. But knowing what you now know, only dimly and in part, surely you realize I've got you over a barrel…ha ha ha, another great Earth expression, no?"

"Try this one on for size: one bad apple spoils the whole barrel."

"Yes, you could be right, Dan, perhaps I really am bad, at least in a lower being's estimation. Ah yes, but consider what an Earth philosopher once said of a fox catching a rabbit: the rabbit says, I hate you! The fox replies, I love you! Still the same old story, right, Dan? Those who claim by right of birth their deserved status as masters, vilified by lessor beings who stand in the way of their triumph. Right, you Absim rabbit?"

"Never had I thought to ever see you, Melzar," Instan slowly replied.

"No doubt, so great an honor to bestow on one of our small ones. Too bad this moment in the end will lose its savor for you. Oh yes, a little sweeping up on this planet seems long overdue to me now. And what better place to start with than its lowest...oh, I tease you, Absim rabbit, I mean lowest in physical stature."

"Fond you are of talking in a condescending way, are you not, Melzar? Funny, beings of a superior kind, I'd thought, not prone to mocking speech."

"Oh, how far off the mark you are, tiny man. Exalted men laugh at the world, have true wit as well they should, a world being their oyster, as some on Dan's home planet would put it."

"No pearl in this oyster for you, Orton, maybe just the grain of dirt you saw fit to implant in it...turns out though you're not a nurturing type, that what needed to grow a cultured pearl."

"And how cultured you imagine yourself, Dan, while knowing little of what you speak. Again a philosopher of your planet once said another true thing, so rare in your parts, when he said all higher culture is based on cruelty, of all things. Imagine that, Dan, a dose of reality for your deluded masses, masses which exist only to serve those few with insight and statecraft."

"Yeah, right. Doesn't take a seer to see what kind of leader you would make."

"*Will* make, Dan. For you see, I know you have my handy globe in your possession. So, I strongly advise you to hand it over. Ah, is that the right Earth expression?"

Before Dan replied, he looked Instan's way. Reading his eyes in a flash, he tossed the orb to Instan, as if a baseball. Then, before Orton could react, Instan tossed the orb onto Orton's right foot. And, rather than squealing with pain, Orton began to spin and then stretch out, contracting as he did to the width of a strand of spaghetti, a strand which stretched high up and down before disappearing from sight.

"Aw man, never thought I'd live to see such things, Instan. It reminded me of what Stephen Hawking once said would happen to a man who fell into a black hole."

"Ah yes, Dan, the reaction in a way like that. Learn Orton did, of some of the powers you spoke of. Oh, and here was his mistake: grasp he failed to do that with the orb a wholly positive force, his visible self, of necessity partly positive but also partly negative, turned entirely negative when the orb struck, inducing his collapse into a patch of dark matter, this instant interaction creating a black hole style vortex."

"How did you learn this?"

"Partly by inhabiting forces he wants to control."

"Huh. Some rabbit. But now, is Orton..."

"Dead? That I cannot say, Dan. And if alive he is, manifold new principles he must swiftly master if he hopes to escape the vortex which consumed him."

"Ah yeah, Stephen Hawking once alluded to tiny black holes appearing and then disappearing...this situation, becoming so obscure now. Ah, but this one thing I know – Orton wanted this orb and came a long way to fetch it. He also took a great risk in creating a visible image of himself. Ah, so his image *only* disappeared into the vortex?"

"Yes and no, Dan. Yes, a self-created image it was of the universally spread out man which disappeared, because his spread out self has vanished into the other side of existing all places at once. By this I mean he now inhabits nowhere only, the exact nature of nowhere, or *nothing*, understood by no one, although suggestions made of it."

"Provoking ideas, Instan. But ah, could he truly inhabit nothing, nothing at all?"

"Oh, my theory imprecise, Dan, as all first theories are. Inhabit now perhaps he does a piece of our universe disappearing into nothing."

"Anything else here, Instan?"

"Yes, a single powerful thought going through Melzar's mind – block the line."

"Block the line, block the line...ha! Could it be that Orton might have been a football player at a long forgotten time in the past?"

"A football player?"

"Oh, just being flippant, Instan, football a game on my planet, played by two equal teams on an equally divided field."

"A force field of some kind?"

"No, just a turf field, just an ordinary game."

"Ah, we also had games."

"Wish this situation were a game. Huh, block the line...on the face of it, just not making sense...and time running out here. Any ideas here, Instan?"

"Ah, well, imagine geometry, Dan."

"Geometry, yeah, line, triangle, hexagon, sphere...okay, we do have a small sphere here...ha! So that clue, possibly relates to this little sphere? And a line of some kind...an imaginary line intersecting with our little sphere...still, just don't see what gives, if we're on the right track, that is."

"More closely consider the sphere, Dan."

"Yeah, well, it's heavy, shiny, like a gem of some kind. Ah, it even has a tiny point of light at its core, so dim it can scarcely be seen...still, it has one dynamic essence."

"I have an idea, Dan. Perhaps its tiny light would grow with more external light?"

"Dunno...wouldn't hurt to try, I guess."

"Let's try using my light."

"Okay, let's take a look at my globe. Ah, brilliant, Instan! Its core looks brighter now…mm, actually getting brighter as we speak…fascinating, in its own small way, but again, who can see the point here? Not me, for one."

Just then though, things began to happen. First, being in a notch between two mountains, one end of the notch facing east and sunrise, light began to grow, but not from the horizon hugging sun. Rather, about thirty degrees above the horizon, a sphere began to shine enough to make its presence felt, even through clouds. As this event unfolded, the globe in Dan's hand also began to shine brightly, this in turn making the mystery sphere beyond the cloud light up even more. But its increased strength was reflected light from the sun, the large mystery sphere acting as a redirecting lens. At first this reflected sunlight shined on Dan's small sphere only, one single beam, this beam forming a straight line of light to the mystery sphere. Next the beam expanded, the entire mountain glowing in its light, light shining through clouds appearing transparent – and then it happened.

"Instan! Did you sense that? Something like this whole dang planet blinking?"

"Yes yes, sense that blink I did, Dan. And now a change in feeling, like after hard rain."

"Yeah, I know that newness feeling, Instan, ozone brought down from up high."

Just as Dan concluded this thought, the sphere moved overhead with a humming sound, more visible now, still shining with dawn light. And then, a wonder few could have foreseen; as the ice orb hovered a moment right overhead, two flecks of light appeared in the sky, clouds now breaking. Simultaneous with this event the orb proceeded westward, but arcing now to the south. Torn between these two wonders, in the end Dan had to watch the tiny flecks of light. Moving at a fair clip, they appeared to be aimed at the mountain. Transfixed by this spectacle,

Dan began to notice what for all the world appeared a kind of flight pattern. Swooping towards the mountain, both objects now banked to the left, putting them on course for the dell they stood in. Dan, beyond fear at this point, could not have budged an inch, even if they had been man sized flying hell toads. And that is what they began to appear as, two men under para-gliders. And so, in that spell bound mood, Dan roared with laughter.

With shouts of alarm and then joy, the two ad hoc eagles took one final bank before hitting a slope not far off, a bit too fast, it appeared. Seeing his cue, Dan bolted up the slope to help his friends, one now snarled in a tree.

"Aw man, what a sight to behold, a truly priceless moment, our world-renowned Captain Grieg held captive by a tree. Ah yeah, and in an improvised para-glider made out of shiny space blankets. Lucky for you this planet only has 1/3 the gravity of Earth."

"Yeah, lucky for us, and lucky for you too, Dan. 'Cause right now I'm pretty damn pissed, might do something I'd later regret if not for this damn tree. So just get me down, double quick, okay?"

"I tend to agree with Dan on this one, Max," Doctor Solander beamed, "this here one rare sight to behold. But no worries, Captain, we'll have you down in a jiffy."

As this scene played out, a bigger one to the south began to unfold. For the mystery sphere of water and ice descended into a sea newly formed, yet a lifeless sea. Lighting up the depths in a marvelous way, new life began to emerge, finding the sea of its birth. Then, further descending into the depths, the melting sphere transposed into life giving currents.

Back on the mountain slope, a reunion unfolded. Led down into the sheltered dell, four men sat in a circle on the comfiest rocks they could find. And so it began, the first stray threads of an unraveled tale weaving themselves back into one fabric.

"Instan," Dan spoke first, "Instan, I do believe you're turning less transparent. Any comment on this welcome development?"

"For the answer look left."

"Aw man, the sun, it's rising! Something cosmic in the works, this planet rotating on its axis now, and here comes the sun! That thing – how did it bring this about?"

"That thing, Dan, as you indelicately put, is both a self-contained aqua-world and type of spacecraft."

"No way! It looked more like some monster sized meteor moving in slow motion."

"A perfectly round shining meteor?"

"Well hey, feel free to fill in the info gaps here."

"I will, with the proviso that we too don't know all the answers here yet. Ah, but since our skipper, on his last dive, made semi-full contact with one of the critters inside it, he should take the podium here."

"Thank you, Doctor Solander. And thank you, Dan, for the rescue…can say that now feeling calmer. Anyhow, do you recall, Dan, that icy thing we noted in the Oort Cloud on the way to Proxima Centauri?"

"No way! You mean to tell me that thing…"

"Yup, one and the same. The hows and whys still foggy for us, this much we know: those, ah, those whales, we decided to call them, them being such in many ways, have been on one long voyage. Ah, but as it turns out, their place of origin is this very planet."

Here all turned to Instan, forcing his cue.

"Oh, yes, well, in the past, behave in more typical ways our planet did, having also seas, two large seas, connected by narrows. Unwanted changes came about when Melzar/Orton struck. Instantly, it appeared, our seas simply vanished, to where we knew not, knowing only seas may disappear with certain powers applied. Those certain powers too froze our planet in space."

"Wait a minute, Instan, that ripple in space-time not far from your planet…might that anomaly be thirty degrees up from the horizon from this spot?"

"How did you know that, Dan?" Captain Grieg cut in. "Because, you know, that's the info relayed to me by one of the whales I learned to communicate with in a mind to mind way. Oh, but he brought it up only in passing, explaining nothing beyond our point of entry. What do *you* know about this?"

"Not a whole lot, Captain, only that it somehow relates to the techno-magic act which froze this planet in space ages ago."

"You mean to tell me that some advanced civilization caused this planet to stand still in space?"

"Well yeah, as Instan just said. And if one of those beings named Orton told us the truth between lies, then a twofold purpose involved: they wanted to study the changes that freezing this planet in its tracks caused for the life here. Ah, but more important, they wanted to see how space-time itself might be altered by such intervention, that nearby ripple in space-time an unexpected but lasting result…ha, which, by the way, is where you guys entered the scene."

"Well, whatever the case with that alien and his story," Doctor Solander cut in, "we did in fact enter the atmosphere here at the thirty degree mark in relation to this spot. Yeah, right on the mark, but only after getting shuck of the most oddball aliens conceivable – funny looking guy just plopped down from out of nowhere."

"Aw now, was he just short of five feet tall, wearing some funky kimono kind of thing, pudgy and sporting some kind of a Mohawk?"

"How the hell did you know that?"

"He's the same nutbar Instan mentioned, the selfsame character we dealt with here and like I just said, his were the people who froze up this planet. But right now I just gotta hear about your encounter."

"Well, Dan, my friend, short it was, and not so sweet...that alien, he looked about ready to turf us out into space without our spacesuits, commandeer our craft."

"Aw man, all so ultra-strange. How'd you get rid of the guy?"

"Well, best we could do was buy ourselves a little time by getting him to look a whale in the eyes, yeah that huge ice orb full of 'em. But their brainwaves, somehow they can transmit 'em mind to mind, hitting like a fist at first, at least for human minds. As for that wackado, it froze him up for a minute. Then, when he came to, the expression on his face read like he'd just received an important long distance call."

"Well, I'll be switched! Possibly at the moment we discovered a little thing he apparently just had to have, this shiny orb."

"Doesn't look like much, Dan."

"No, but it's close cousin to the large metallic sphere he once lived in on this very planet, in fact."

"I sense a major saga in the making here, Dan. Think the captain and me both need a rest before hearing it all. And I mean to tell ya, talk about your adrenaline rushes, oh yeah, our paraglide from this planet's upper atmosphere...damn! Float like a butterfly, sting like a bee, to borrow the words of one great boxer."

"Yeah, and a ride like that – really takes it out of a man. But could you tell me, at least, how you arrived here riding that sphere from thousands of light years away."

"Ah yeah, thousands of light years away...but now, as to how an ice coated drop of a sea arrived here in such a jiffy, well now, son, that I could not tell you."

"Huh, great, leaving us with Aashi's imaginary premise as a guiding light."

"Imaginary premise?"

"Well yeah, you know, conjecture based on images the mind conjures up when studying mathematical problems. Consider, for example, how some noted theorists, seeing the solution to a mathematical problem in images first, would then transcribe them into mathematical constructs. And you know, this planet's wonky sidewise poles affected our dreams, making us dream more vivid than before, in the end aiding this process."

"You don't say? Both beautiful dreamers now, that about the size of it?"

"Right. But now, as for Aashi's contribution to our understanding of this planet, well, I'll leave that story for her to tell once you guys have rested up."

"And in the meantime?"

"In the meantime, Doc, picking up the imagine knack too, I played around with it."

"So okay, Dan, let's hear what you have to say here before I knock your knack."

"Right. So let me see, if we had an opening in that anomaly, that ripple in space-time, a tear opening up in it, then you guys arrived here by barreling right through it."

"Sounds like a real air sandwich, Dan," Captain Grieg cut in. "Just consider the fact that the distance we travelled from the Oort Cloud to here is thousands of light years. Oh ho, wait, it's finally registering with me now that I've calmed down. We *did* in fact just travel, on that ice ball, no less, thousands of light years in a matter of, huh, so short a time it lasted about one blink…sheer nonsense! No damn way it can be but it is…please proceed with your theory, Dan."

"Okay, but more a bare bone thought than full blown theory. So yeah, a rip in the fabric of space-time means that nothing, *literally*, stands between one rip and another…nothing there, no transit time involved in arriving at the next rip."

"Ha! Now I need a drink or three, that bit about two rips making some kind of sense. Bad news, crew. We've all been in space way too long."

"Ah," Doctor Solander spoke up, "then if we somehow entered a rip in space-time and were shunted to this here rip, then presto! here we are. But now, it couldn't have just happened by accident, us entering a rare tear like that, and then on through another, way too complex an accident...leading me to suspect that ice coated raindrop of a spacecraft had some way of inducing a much needed rip at our former location."

"Yes," Instan piped in, "no accident it could have been. And your orb, Dan, some role to play it had, lighting up the way as it did."

"Dan's orb, yeah right," Captain Grieg grinned. "Always wanted to rule a planet of your own, right Dan?"

"He means this here little bauble, Captain Grieg."

"What the hell is it? Ball bearing of some kind?"

"You know, Captain, I'm not gonna just slough off that comment...'cause ah, this object did, in a sense, insure the smooth working of other moving parts...ah, but more concretely, it comes from the much larger orb that alien lived in. He claimed it appeared spontaneously when the rip in space-time opened up during their experiment, that rip an unforeseen result. He further claimed it came from somewhere inside of that break in space-time, it not having been made by his people."

"Damn. Another orb. Composed of?"

"Some unknown metallic alloy, at least appearance wise. But it had an elastic, changeable quality to it, plus latent energy of some sort."

"Of super proportions, no doubt."

"No doubt. It arrested the alien's aging process, for one thing, amplified his own personal powers, for another."

"Anything else?"

"Yeah, he could project his brainwaves, or some facsimile of his presence, to other places, onto the center of this planet's night side, for example."

"Just like that, eh? Presto chango."

"Well hey, nothing works in a normal way on this planet, at least until now – this unexplained restoration of Planet Alcenta's former conditions. What gives here? So your ice-coated water sphere barrels through a rip in space-time…how did that act to set this process in motion?"

"Haven't a clue on that one, Dan. Ah, but what about your damn orbs? What happened to the big one? And how'd you end up with the little one?"

"The big one vanished when the alien left it."

"And the small one?"

"It came from inside the big one. At first we thought it destroyed with the main one, but then Instan found it not far from here. As to the role it played in this cosmic drama, well, it's a mystery to me…although my new theory of…no, wait. I'll save that for later. A little too convoluted for now, and you guys so tired."

"Well now, if Aashi were here, would she not spin an imaginary yarn to at least give us some food for thought? And you have that knack too, right?"

"Right…and that two rips in space-time theory, something to think about, along with the smoke and mirrors act ages ago that froze up this planet, and the unknown water drop spacecraft turning up in deep space inside the Oort Cloud…and the functions of this here small orb…and that Orton character, he tried to stop this um, this lining up of objects from occurring."

"But why, Dan?"

"Because it somehow acted to orient your ice sphere's reentry."

"That's it! Just reached my info overload point."

"Ah yes, which means we need to trek to an encampment not far from this mountain. Aashi's there, plus others you'd like to meet, after mulling this quakin' 8.5 cosmic event."

And so, down the mountain they went on into Olkar's encampment, unopposed by hordes of frenzied leptons. For now with the sun coming up, those small enough scurried for cover, toads and toad-like creatures averse to the sun. The larger ones worst hit, they tried to retreat to a night side no long in existence. In either case, both large and small had lost their aggression.

Olkar, happy to see them, beamed and shook hands, liking this custom Dan taught him. Then of course a herbal drink was served as all got acquainted. Happy to be back with Aashi, Dan sipped tea with her, both calmly smiling. The extent of this cosmic event slow to seep in, to his amazement, Dan missed the static dawn effect, at least for a moment. For it had given him pause on the topic of time, and had brought with it an odd sense of peace. Now though, that great cosmic clock was running again, and soon on this planet people would be running with it as well. For with this great event came greater expectations. These long isolated peoples would now strive to once more erect a thriving civilization, with all its clear advantages along with the pitfalls. And time would mark their daily life with the silent tick-tock of changing shadows. No more sense of being poised on a wave.

Next day, Dan sat on the edge of camp noting its high-spirited mood. Next turning to the mountain, he began to immerse himself in recent events. With time and space enough alone, bits and pieces of the puzzle began to fall into place.

"Ah yes, Aashi told me I would find you here."

"Bretori!" Dan exclaimed, jumping up to embrace his friend. "Bretori! Well, my God, what a sight for sore eyes! Aha, and now I know something big hatched in the process we uncovered here, but um, understand only in fragments."

"My people too, Dan, understand our cosmos only in fragments."

"Aw now, don't be modest, Bretori, a fragment for you a major chunk for us. And I suspect you know a lot of behind the scenes info about the recent events here."

"Some certain pieces of the mosaic, yes, I do know. But Dan, you are an agent of independent thought and action. This being so, in the unfolding events here, you have learned much."

"Yeah, but I'd have–"

"Ah, an expression your people use, Dan, no buts."

"Ifs or ands. But *that,* Bretori, presupposes a keen and uploaded mind, a mind well advanced beyond imagination based conjecture."

"Pause a moment, Dan, and picture the events which you have seen here. Picture them one by one, pause, and connecting the pictures, tell me what emerges here."

"A major task, Bretori, for one person alone…and so much of what we *think* happened here based on Aashi's new, um, new theory of imaginary waves, angles, and so on…so I have to give her major credit. Later, when we all gather together, best to let her run her scenario by you."

"Ah yes, you wish to put your spouse before yourself, an admirable impulse. But tell me now what you were thinking as I walked up. Tell me that much right now, at least."

"Fair enough, Bretori. So okay, right before you walked up, first I'd thought about the sphere nestled in that mountain dell Aashi and me found. Now, at first we supposed it had been destroyed somehow, when Orton bounded out of it, vaporized, or something like that, because appearance-wise it simply vanished. Ah, but now, what if it had bolted at lightning speed back through a newly ripped hole in the fabric of space-time?"

"What if it had? Tell me its tale as you see it, had that occurred."

"Okay. So first, it transits through…nothing, nothing being what exists, or ah, doesn't exist? with space-time taken out of the picture. Next the sphere emerged through another such rip…ah, and of course transiting through nothing does not involve time. So, it could just as well have emerged thousands of light years away as it could a short ways off. And ah, that ice coated water drop of a spacecraft, so many thousands of light years from here, maybe that the spot."

"So you suppose a random rip in space-time near the icy orb?"

"Well, that is remotely possible, Bretori."

"Tell me of this remote possibility."

"Well, okay, suppose that…ah, wait a minute, something more likely than that might have occurred. That major sphere of ours on this planet, we all sensed hidden powers…so that same orb tore a *new* hole in space-time at a location of its choosing, in this case by that strange water spacecraft."

"The orb was drawn to water?"

"No, not water, ice, a twenty-five mile wide orb of ice…that, I now suppose, what we all saw while travelling through the Oort Cloud to Proxima Centauri. And then, the mystery sphere from this planet *merged* with that ice ball, forming the core of its core, and so providing just enough heat to thaw it out mostly, while preserving a thick layer of ice all around. And the life within, those whales and other living things…had been preserved in ice for ages, maybe. You know of cryogenics, the freezing of living things to be thawed out and revived later – this the state that strange orb was in when Captain Grieg and Doctor Solander landed on it…and the spin the doctor told me of, yeah, to provide a bit of gravity, needed for the proper preservation of higher lifeforms, even frozen.

"And then that newly empowered water sphere ripped a new hole in space-time and presto! It emerged again near this planet, right in that ripple of space-time which has persisted for ages. So next it floats like a spacecraft right over this planet, getting lower…ha, then the escapade of the para-glider jump…I'll leave that bit for our captain and doctor to tell you about…yes, and their instantaneous trek through nothing, although they have no recollection of it."

"Any other thoughts?"

"Yeah, how, how had all this been arranged? If in fact it proves to be the case? Maybe, just maybe, it happened that way…aha! And maybe, just maybe, the whale and sea orb was contained in the sphere as it newly appeared in this world ages ago! After the Melzar attack…making said orb a seed of sorts to plant in the future."

"An intriguing notion, Dan. But gaps exist in your account. First, if the orb acted to preserve this planet's seas when it first appeared through cryogenics, how did the frozen ball end up in deep space? Second, why did the sphere not act right after the initial planetary disruption to restore the seas as well as the planet's normal behavior?"

"Ah yeah…but let me start with issue two. It might be true that Orton's entry into the sphere somehow froze up its actions, his presence merging to a point with its works."

"Then why did not the sphere restore the seas right away when Orton finally left it?"

"Oh, well, because, Bretori, it had long ago propelled that sea life lifeboat into deep space, to protect the lives it contained from Orton's interference, should he have discovered the seas stored inside, in some miniaturized way? Some non-space-time dependent way? Ah, and furthermore, since the ice orb appeared more or less headed for Earth when we spotted it in the Oort Cloud, might not Earth's seas have been its life preserving goal?"

"Yes, perhaps the whales could have been genetically modified to allow for such a transition, if other options failed to materialize."

"Well now, could be with Melzar gone the sphere had to fetch its lost seas for restoration…ah, so the backup option of landing that ice orb on Earth was ruled out."

"That sounds possible, Dan."

"Right. Anyway, our ice seas' primary goal was a return to *this* planet…supposing normal planetary behavioral, rotation and orbit and all could be restored…this restoration blocked by an alien presence within the sphere itself, a hostile alien presence."

"And with the sphere's absolutely benign nature, it could not act against even Orton's errant behavior. In truth, it acted to preserve his life through time."

"Yeah, okay, Bretori, I'll buy that. So then, with Orton gone, out the sphere went through another rip in space-time right near that longstanding warp in space-time near this planet. Next, and as I just said, by merging with that tiny ice world, becoming the core of its core, it radiated just enough heat to thaw it out mostly, while preserving the ice shell…then it revived those dormant sea creatures…this the state Captain Grieg and Doctor Solander found the ice sphere in. And then, of course, the sphere brought about a reverse transit through the nothingness beyond space-time, it having the power to rip another hole in said space-time…but why go to all this trouble to preserve a sea and its life?"

"You tell me, Dan."

"Well, because, um, because one of the first effects of the halting of this planet's normal cycles had in some inexplicable way induced the disappearance of its seas, meaning all life in them likely extinguished…so the sphere preserved that glob of the sea with its life, knowing land creatures would survive in this planet's new condition, but not so sea creatures. Oh, but what the heck happened to the seas here? Where did they go?"

"They merged with a vast cloud of ice crystals surrounding our galaxy, like a mammoth version of the Oort Cloud you mentioned. All terrestrial seas had their origin in this cloud in a more formative stage of our galaxy's development, when its shape was spherical, not the spiral of today."

"Really? So *why* did this planet's seas transpose to there, so far away?"

"Because the disruption in space-time brought on by Orton's malicious fellows for an instant put this planet back at a stage when it had no seas, meaning those former seas instantly transposed to the cloud they had come from. But then that moment passed, leaving all else the same. And now, the sphere's return to this planet involved a *reverse* course through that space-time disturbance. You see, Dan, when the sphere was originally propelled into deep space to protect the sea creatures, that *forward* course accompanied the process that would strip this planet of its seas. So what we recently witnessed, the sphere on a reverse course from its original escape course – it represents a reversal of the split second in which the seas had disappeared. This means that a re-transposition of the seas from the extra-galactic cloud was forced, right at the moment movement was restored to this planet…but lifeless seas which our returning water orb next seeded with life. And furthermore, that was also the *primary* reason it projected the sea ice sphere into deep space, a reverse journey a necessary precondition for not just the seas' return, but for the overall restoration of this dysfunctional planet."

"So Orton's former sphere…just a seed of sea life!"

"Yes, true, yet with manifold other functions."

"Yeah, we supposed as much. But now, what might some of those other functions be?"

"You are not prepared at this time, Dan, to learn of those functions."

"Okaaay...hey, wait a minute! Where might that sphere be right now?"

"In your hand."

"What? You mean contained in this little sphere?"

"Size is irrelevant for the forces we speak of, Dan."

"What should I do with it?"

"We will speak of this later."

"And so, Aashi and me, our break in...turns out to be what needed?"

"Yes, Dan, as unlikely as it sounds. My people – yes, we tried to lure Orton out of the sphere right from the start, heal the planet back then. But he sensed the need to remain inside its safe and spacious confines, a man with an infinite shell."

"Yeah, a shell of a man with a shell. Wait, the whales – way intelligent beyond the norm."

"Living in the sphere caused that."

"Okay, alright, but now, that sphere...where the heck did it come from? Did some uber-advanced beings make it?"

"Coming from beyond space-time, Dan, we cannot speak of in terms of the sphere being made, things being made in time, in a material order, not *in* nothing."

"Not *in* nothing? But out of nothing? Matter in our universe coming into being out of nothing?"

"Some say this is true, as you well know. But our sphere *came* from nothing already in the solid appearing form we know and see. Yes, nothing, which is, as an Earth scientist once said, the possibility of everything."

"Ha, yeah, nothing to it! This whole mess."

"But Dan, your improvised theory of Orton's new powers. Can you explain why the sphere, sharing that same power of Orton's to be everywhere and nowhere at the same time, did not simply manifest itself by the ice/water orb from that endless presence, instead of remaining in one substantial form to move though space-time?"

"Ah yeah...well now, Bretori, might it be due to the fact that its nowhere/everywhere presence, like an electron spinning around an atomic nucleus, in a very real sense exists as a probability only. And what needed for this planetary transformation act was something more, um, grounded in the material universe? Since planetary restoration would fall under that rubric? So a more material, at least to look at, manifestation called for?"

"Yes, something of that nature, Dan."

"But now we have to factor in that Melzar/Orton."

"Yes we do, Dan. And your improvised theory concerning Orton – it allowed you to ever so slightly edge out that dangerous being."

"Is he gone? Is he dead?"

"Yes and no, Dan."

"Oh boy, *that* trick line again. Ah, but his landing on the ice/water sphere – his onetime sphere at its core...so he planned to live within it again?"

"In a sense, yes, but in a different state, *both* existing everywhere and nowhere at the same time, a powerful combination."

"He did want power. So why didn't he enter the sphere while on the ice globe?"

"Because the sphere's positive aura repelled his presence, once he made a move toward it, and that at the moment he made eye contact with the whale. But the whale, quite intelligent – it tricked him into making his move, so activating the sphere's resistance. And then, as Orton perceived the small orb here on this planet turning active again, a much easier target for him, or so he thought, he decided to come to this planet. You see, Dan, so new to his vast powers, Orton hadn't thought through every implication of what he did. One could say that Orton's first bold manifestation of his new self was tried out too soon.

As to exactly where he is now, and whether he will be back, even I have no answer to that. For now he inhabits nowhere alone."

"Nowhere alone…got a pretty desolate ring to it. Wait a minute, nowhere…is not the same as nothing? Nowhere relating to the material order, nothing to what beyond it?"

"I'll allow you to ponder that question alone, Dan."

"Great. But now, how did that negative Orton gain entry into the sphere in the first place?"

"Yes, how *did* he gain that entry do you think?"

"Dunno, Bretori, a real mystery here…ah, but let me dip into some of Aashi's treasured impressions…yeah, might it be that at first the orb's beauty for a moment overwhelmed him, causing a positive aura to envelop even his hateful being?"

"Yes, Dan, something as simple as a being's love of beauty and the positive energy it generates may explain his easy first entry. True to say that no being commences life misaligned inside. Aberrations of that nature come later, are learned traits, not inherent in any known race of beings."

"Huh, yeah, a simple love of beauty, so basic to our existence and yet so often overlooked as a motivating force. Sad, real sad, what happened to Orton's people…and you know what? Even though that guy deserved what he got in spades, I sure don't feel triumphant…almost pain I feel for him now, as odd as that sounds."

Bretori studied Dan for a moment and smiled.

"That feeling, Dan, is what separates us from malevolent beings. And, while justice demanded what Orton received, we may still pity him in a way."

"Well heck, had to be that way for us to be, and to get this planet restored. Aw man, and the gush of life here now…what a sight for sore eyes."

"Yes, Dan, a sight for sore eyes."

About John Albrecht

Born in St. Boniface, Manitoba, Canada, as a child my family moved to San Diego, California, where I grew up. Later attending the University of New Mexico, I graduated with a BA in Psychology, minor in history. Moving then to Toronto, Canada, I obtained a qualification for teaching English as a second language and next spend a number of years teaching English in the Republic of Korea. There I rediscovered the beauty of both sculpting and writing, always my true passions. Back in Canada then, with a budding interest in cosmology this story took shape.

Acknowledgements

This being my first publication, I must begin by going all the way back to my 4th grade teacher, Mr. Petka. A gifted teacher who wanted his pupils to love learning for its own sake, he encouraged me with my writing. Next, I would like to thank Leah Wilson, coworker and friend, for her vitality and willingness to share new impressions. Professor Hwang in Korea, employer and friend, also encouraged me with my writing. Gena Sze, whom I met at an employment agency, gave me a boost at a difficult time by asking me what my dream was. I would also like to thank my friend Mike Duffy for our correspondence. We have shared many ideas and he has reviewed some of my writing. He too is now thinking of writing on various topics. Nora Mader, a writer herself, had time and patience enough to teach me, among other things, the value of developing an eye for self-editing. Her brother, Al Mader, also a friend of mine involved with writing, encouraged me with my work.

Made in the USA
Coppell, TX
06 June 2021

56931038R00105